THE FAR HORIZON

THE FAR HORIZON

Anne Forsyth

CHIVERS

British Library Cataloguing in Publication Data available

This Large Print edition published by AudioGO Ltd, Bath, 2013.
Published by arrangement with the Author

U.K.   Hardcover   ISBN   978 1 4713 1653 1
U.K.   Softcover   ISBN   978 1 4713 1654 8

Printed and bound in Great Britain by
MPG Books Group Limited

FIFE, 1822

'This can't be the right place!' Eliza glared at the coachman. 'I thought it was a mansion. This is nothing like a mansion.'

He spat out of the window without glancing round at her.

'That was my orders, miss,' he said contemptuously.

'I am certainly not going to stay there,' Eliza said. 'You can just turn around and take me back!'

He sat not moving.

'I was telt to bring you here.'

Eliza drew her shawl more tightly round herself and shivered. She hardly glanced at the waves crashing over the low wall. The coach had turned off the main road into a narrow lane—there were only a few fishermen's cottages and one tall house. Once it had been an important house, no doubt, but now it stood alone among the poor dilapidated cottages. The red roof tiles, brought by sea from Holland, had shattered and broken tiles lay on the ground.

'I cannot be expected to stay there,' Eliza said firmly. 'I was told it was a grand house.'

'That's as may be. I'm no' going back again,' the coach driver said. He clambered down from his seat and took Eliza's valise from the

1

back of the coach. 'There you are,' he said.

'I'm not staying here.' Eliza's voice rose.

'Please yourself, miss.'

'How can I carry my valise?' Eliza stood her ground.

He shook his head.

'I had my orders,' he said. And he clicked his tongue at the grey horse and turned about to make his way back up the hill.

'You can't leave me here,' Eliza called shrilly after him, but her words were lost in the gusts of wind that swept them away over the sea wall.

She stood alone in the empty lane.

I could burst into tears, she thought. But that would have done no good. Besides, Eliza was not the kind of girl much given to tears. Instead she became angry. In a rage she tried to lift the heavy bag that held all her possessions, her clothes and one or two precious books, and began to make her way, stumbling, towards the house.

'Are ye needin' a hand?'

Eliza turned round.

'Where did you come from?' She gazed, astonished, at the sign of some human life in this desolate place—and here was a boy who seemed to have sprung from nowhere. She had thought she was quite alone in the lane.

'I'm waitin' for the boats comin' back,' he said.

She looked at him. Although it was a cold

2

evening, he wore only a tattered jersey and a pair of trousers that were much too large for him, and his boots were out at the toes. But he had a cheerful, impudent expression and seemed to take no notice of the weather.

'Are you gaun' to Shore House?'

She nodded.

'I'll cairry yer bag.'

Eliza hesitated, wondering if such a small boy could manage to lift it, but he swung it up with no difficulty and set off the few yards up the lane. Eliza didn't know what to do. The carrier who had brought her here had vanished, and she knew no-one in this village—no-one in this part of Fife. And here she was quite alone, but for a grubby urchin whose accent she could hardly understand.

Despite her misery Eliza could see the funny side. She began to laugh as she fumbled in her purse for a coin.

'Here you are,' she said as he set the bag down in front of the house. He stretched out his hand, took the coin and turned it over in his hand, looking at it a little suspiciously

'I'll be away, then.'

'Here, wait a moment. What do they call you?'

'Just Robbie.' His voice floated back to her. 'Anything you want, just you ask for me, miss. Folks know me around here.'

'Thank you.' So she wasn't quite alone. Eliza looked up at the house. She had little

3

idea what to expect.

She squared her shoulders. There was nothing for it.

'I can't stand here all night,' she said to herself, shivering.

The brass door knocker in the shape of a fish needed a good clean, she noticed. It clearly hadn't been polished for some time. She knocked a couple of times at the heavy black door and waited impatiently. It was no night to be waiting in the street. Suddenly she felt overwhelmed by the darkness, the ferocity of the storm and the bleak loneliness of this place. Her boots were not waterproof and the hem of her skirt was soaked. Eliza was angry now—why didn't they answer?

She knocked again, more loudly.

A few moments later she could hear stumbling footsteps. There was the sound of a key turning in the lock and the door was opened a few inches.

'And what would you be wanting?' The woman who stood there was dressed entirely in black. She had a coarse rasping voice and she refused to open the door wider.

'I'm expected,' Eliza said. 'Miss Eliza Dunlop from Edinburgh. Am I to wait outside in the storm or be admitted?'

The woman looked suspicious.

'You'd better come in,' she said after a moment's hesitation.

'Thank you.' Eliza picked up her valise and

4

entered the house.

*   *   *

It had all begun about a month ago in Edinburgh. For a year or two Eliza had been companion, maid and general dogsbody to a cantankerous old woman. Miss Gregory lived in a large and very inconvenient house in the New Town.

'I am, of course, gentry,' she never tired of reminding Eliza. 'My father was a writer to the signet.' Eliza didn't know what this was, but she knew it must be important as her employer was clearly proud of her late father. But, oh, she was difficult. Fifty times a day, it seemed, she would have Eliza running up the stairs to the top of the house to bring various items to her.

Sometimes Eliza would have liked to say sharply, 'Fetch it yourself', but she knew she didn't dare—she would have been dismissed right away. And where else could she go?

She had no family, her parents having died of cholera some years before. Eliza had been brought up by an aunt—a pleasant, though somewhat remote person, absorbed in books, spending most of her time writing letters of complaint to the government, the royal family, and anyone of the slightest importance. Eliza had been fond of her eccentric relative, and missed her when she died a few years

5

usly.

Edinburgh in the early 19th century,
; was little enough choice for a girl on
own. She could be a governess, or work
ı companion. If there was nothing else, she
ıld go into service, or perhaps find work in
ıe mills.

'I hate being an orphan,' she told herself
rebelliously. 'I hate always being poor Eliza.'

For a time she had lived with her cousin,
William, and his wife. The wife was a sharp-
tongued shrew, who treated Eliza like a
servant. William regarded his cousin as just
another mouth to feed, and often complained,
in Eliza's hearing, of what it cost to give her a
home under his roof.

It was a relief when William heard of the
post of companion to old Miss Gregory, and
before she knew what was happening, Eliza
was bundled out of the house, with her valise
containing her Sunday dress and shawl, and a
few other precious possessions.

Now, though Eliza disliked working for the
old lady, there was at least a half-day off every
week. As soon as she could, she escaped from
the gloomy house in Heriot Row and walked
to George Street, where she would watch
the crowds, especially the fashionable ladies,
strolling up and down. Oh, she often thought,
if only I had a silk dress like that, admiring
an elegant gown in peppermint green stripes
and a bonnet trimmed with bright ribbons.

And then she would escape into her favourite daydream.

In this dream Eliza had a choice of elegant dresses—her favourite, she decided, was a creamy silk dress in the fashionable Empire line. It was studded with embroidered yellow rosebuds and there was a net fichu around her shoulders. Perhaps she would wear a velvet mantle, trimmed with fur, and maybe a swansdown muff. A parasol, definitely.

'I would have the most elegant gloves,' she decided. 'Long, white gloves.'

In her dream there was a handsome young man—fair hair or dark curly hair, she couldn't decide. But he was the most handsome man in the whole of the city, she was sure of that, as he stopped before her and swept off his top hat in greeting.

'Here, mind yourself, miss!' A lad with a barrow crammed with vegetables skidded to a halt behind her.

Eliza's daydream vanished as a bag of potatoes cascaded to the pavement.

'You should watch where you're going,' the lad grumbled.

Eliza stepped aside in as dignified a way as she could. If the handsome young escort had been by her side, he would have spoken sharply to the boy.

'How dare you address a lady like that?'

But when you were an orphan, poor and shabbily dressed, Eliza thought, abandoning her daydream, you had to hold your tongue.

There was no company in the house, except for the cook and the housemaid. The housemaid, Ida, did as little as she could, and slipped out every night to meet her lad, the carpenter's apprentice, on the corner of the street. She took hardly any notice of Eliza.

One day, Eliza thought, I will go out of this house and never come back. I might sail away from Leith, perhaps to Norway. I might take the coach from Edinburgh and travel through the night to England. I might meet a young man who would help me escape.

Her dreams were interrupted by the clanging of the old lady's bell. She sighed and hurried upstairs to see what her employer wanted now.

'Make sure the fire in the drawing-room is stoked. And see that there is claret and glasses, and plain biscuits—Mr Humbie is coming to visit me this afternoon.' The old lady glanced at the watch pinned to the bodice of her black silk. 'At three o'clock?'

'Yes, ma'am.' Eliza sighed inwardly and hurried off. Mr Humbie, the lawyer, visited Miss Gregory at least once a month. He would sip a glass of claret, munch a plain biscuit and dust the crumbs from his trousers, before fitting his spectacles on his nose.

'Now to business, dear lady,' he would say. At this point Eliza was dismissed, but usually she heard enough to know that her employer was about to change her will yet again.

Sometimes it was the fund for foundlings that was out of favour. Another week she had tired of supporting foreign missions and wished instead to give her money to poor gentlewomen.

'Quite so, dear lady.' Eliza hated the sound of his oily tones. He was very polite to Miss Gregory, but he always ignored Eliza, except for one occasion, when she had dropped his hat. As she'd handed it to him, he had snapped crossly at her, 'You careless girl—give me that.' And he'd fussily polished the crown of his hat, taking no notice of her apologies.

But then, after a short illness, the old lady died and everything changed, it seemed, overnight.

'And what's going to happen I don't know,' Cook said.

The housemaid was not concerned.

'There's plenty other jobs going,' she said airily.

Eliza was at a loss. She had no idea how to go about finding another job, unless, she thought, she were to go and knock at the doors of some of the grand houses round Charlotte Square. There was no use asking cousin William for help, she decided. He had made it quite clear that once she had taken the post with the old lady, she need not expect anything more from him.

But what could she do, she wondered.

9

The day after Miss Gregory's funeral, she was still undecided about her future, when there was a message from the lawyer.

She was to call at his office, on the North Bridge, at three o'clock precisely on the following day.

Eliza was greatly cheered by this. Surely the old lady must have remembered her in that frequently changed will. What would it be? A piece of jewellery, perhaps? Books, maybe. No, Eliza decided reluctantly, that wasn't very likely. In the two years she had worked for Miss Gregory she had never been thanked for anything she had done.

However, she darned her stockings, and polished her shoes, and put on her Sunday dress of plain grey wool. Her black bonnet would have to do. She would dearly have loved to trim it with a ribbon, perhaps one in cornflower blue, but no, she decided that would not be appropriate. She was, after all, supposed to be in mourning for her late employer, though so far, Eliza had not mourned the old lady to any great extent.

It was a fine day and Eliza enjoyed the walk in the sunshine. She made her way along George Street, then crossed Princes Street. Along the length of the North Bridge, skirting the markets.

She looked carefully at the address she had been given in Hunter Square, near the Tron Church, just opposite the coach stand. Yes, here was the building.

She climbed the stairs to the first floor and waited in the oak-panelled ante-room. She could hear voices inside, and after a few moments, a tall, swarthy man burst out of the office and, without looking at her, clattered down the stairs.

What was the matter, Eliza wondered—had he had a quarrel with the lawyer? Something about a family will, perhaps? She was absorbed in her thoughts when the door to the office opened again and Mr Humbie looked out at her.

'Come in, miss.'

She sat down in the chair he indicated, and for a moment there was silence. From the other side of a large desk the lawyer looked at her, pursing his lips.

Then he said, 'You have been with Miss Gregory—let me see . . .'

'Two years, sir,' Eliza interrupted.

'Two years, yes.' He paused.

'Well, I expect you will be looking for another situation.' Suddenly he smiled at her, and Eliza found this very disconcerting. He was clearly not used to smiling—he bared his long yellow teeth in what was more like a snarl than a smile. 'I have the very thing for you.'

'Oh.' Eliza was disappointed. It was not to be a pendant then, or a sum of money. Mean old woman, she thought.

'A companion to a young lady,' he said,

11

sounding impressive.

'Oh:'Eliza wasn't sure about this. She was tired of being a companion—running up and downstairs at the whim of some employer and being blamed for everything that went wrong. Never having any fun, no laughter.

'It is a very good post,' the lawyer went on. 'You are fortunate.' He took a pinch of snuff from a silver snuffbox, and peered over his spectacles at Eliza.

'Where is it to be? In Edinburgh?' Eliza asked.

'No. In Fife. In a fine house in Kingsferry.'

'I've never heard of it,' Eliza said. She had a vague idea it was somewhere near Anstruther, in the East Neuk of Fife.

'That makes no odds,' the lawyer said impatiently. 'The young lady in question has arrived recently from the Low Countries. She is not in the best of health, and is in need of a companion. You will do very well. And the sea air at Kingsferry will do her good.'

'I don't think—' Eliza began.

'You are not being paid to think, miss,' the lawyer told her. 'It has all been arranged. You will get your board and a wage, and you will set off on Friday morning for Leith, then will cross to Inverkeithing and from there you will travel by coach. A passage has been arranged.'

'And who . . .' Eliza gulped, hardly able to take in all this information '. . . and who will be my employer if I take this post?'

'Hoity-toity.' The lawyer sniffed. 'As I said, miss, you are not in a position to decide whether or not you will take the position. I assume you have no other employer in mind— no-one clamouring for your services, eh?' He attempted a grin, and Eliza closed her eyes.

'No,' she said after a few moments. 'But I am sure . . .'

'You have no choice,' the lawyer said firmly. 'And as for who your employer will be, that is a secret and will remain so.' He went on. 'You will pack up your belongings and a carriage will call for you on Friday morning at ten o'clock. Make sure you are ready. You will cross to Fife by ferry and a carriage will be waiting to take you to Kingsferry.' He turned back to the papers on his desk.

'But—' Eliza began.

'No buts, miss,' he said sharply.

'May I ask one question, then?' Eliza said.

'Yes?' He glared at her.

'How am I to be paid?' Eliza asked. She was determined not to be intimidated by the lawyer.

He sniffed.

'Your wages will be sent to you at the beginning of each month. Minus what you owe for your board.'

'You mentioned,' Eliza stood her ground, 'my board and wage. So my board should not be taken out of my earnings. I could,' she said, greatly daring, 'earn more elsewhere. I have,

13

after all, been a companion to Miss Gregory for two years, and she had no fault to find with me.'

The lawyer sniffed again.

'I have laid down the terms, miss. However, your board will be paid, over and above your wages.' He opened a drawer and rummaged in a cash box. 'Here,' he said, 'is some money for your expenses until you are paid.' He turned back to the papers on his desk. 'I am, as you see, a very busy man. Good day to you.'

I have won that round, Eliza thought, and she felt pleased with herself.

She rose to go. There were dozens of questions she wanted to ask, but she knew it would be a waste of time.

On the way back to the grim house in Heriot Row she began to feel a little more cheerful. After all, she'd never been to Fife. It would be somewhere different. And perhaps the young lady would be an interesting companion. Eliza always looked on the bright side.

At least, she told herself, as she pushed open the heavy oak door, she need never enter this house again.

Her spirits rose and she found herself almost looking forward to her new life.

On Monday morning she needed all her optimism. After a fine sunny spell, the weather had turned stormy—it might as well be autumn instead of summer, she thought despondently, gazing out of the window. The rain battered the windows of the carriage as she peered out. On the quay at Leith, she tried to find a shelter, clutching her shawl around her and trying to prevent her bonnet from blowing away in a gust of wind.

When the steam packet arrived at last, she felt thankful. At least there will be some sort of shelter, she thought. But no sooner had the boat left the harbour than she realised that it was going to be a stormy crossing—the waves thundered against the sides of the ferry, and the boat began to rise above the waves, then plunge downwards again.

Eliza shivered and began to feel queasy. If only the ferry would turn back. Even the miserable surroundings of Leith would be better than this. She clutched the rail, desperately peering into the mist, trying to see the coastline ahead. But the fog was so thick that she could see nothing at all. Surely this couldn't go on for ever?

A thought suddenly struck Eliza. She was quite alone in the world. No-one knew where she was except that lawyer in Edinburgh. If she perished on this voyage, there was no-one to care. No-one at all.

Strangely enough, she was somewhat comforted by this thought. She pulled her cloak around her, and decided she would not give way to self-pity. There was a new life ahead.

Eliza clutched the rail more tightly, and with

the distraction of these ideas, began to feel more cheerful.

When at last the boat berthed in Inverkeithing, Eliza stumbled off, her hair lank beneath her bonnet, which had been sorely battered by the wind. She was pale and shivering and, despite her good resolutions, longed for nothing so much as a warm fire and a hot meal.

Instead, there was the coach, shabby and in need of a coat of paint, and the surly coachman who did not even try to help her with her valise.

Eliza had sunk back against the moth-eaten cushions that smelled of damp.

This was the beginning of her new life.

A COMPANION

As soon as she stepped over the threshold later in the afternoon, Eliza knew that she needn't expect warmth and comfort here.

'I would like to wash and change my clothes,' Eliza said firmly, indicating her wet skirts.

'Oh, aye?' The woman who had opened the door seemed quite uninterested.

'At once,' Eliza said firmly.

'Your room's up the stair.' The woman led the way up a creaking stair. She paused on the landing and then began, with a sigh, to climb the second flight.

'This'll be your room,' she said.

It was small and poky, but Eliza was thankful to see it was fairly clean, and the bedding on the iron bedstead was at least dry. There was a small chest of drawers, on which stood a pewter candlestick, and an upright chair. There was nowhere to hang her clothes, but Eliza decided she would make some arrangement later on. There were no pictures in the bleak little room, not even a framed text on the wall. But for the moment she was too hungry to think of anything else but a good meal.

'You'll get your dinner downstairs in the dining-room,' the woman said. 'We eat early here.'

'And you are?' Eliza asked.

'I'm the housekeeper,' the woman admitted reluctantly.

'And your name . . .' Eliza probed.

'I'm Mistress Kilbain,' the woman returned unsmilingly.

'I'm sure we'll get along fine,' Eliza said, trying to sound optimistic. 'And the young lady?' she went on. 'When do I meet her?'

'She'll be taking her dinner with you,' Mistress Kilbain said, before she turned and went downstairs.

Well, this is a strange place I've come to, Eliza thought. Maybe it will look very much better in the morning, with the sun out, and the gulls whirling round the harbour, and the fishing boats coming in to land.

Eliza changed her skirt and tried to untangle her curls. But at last she gave it up, and made her way downstairs. On the way, on the first floor, she peeped into what was clearly the drawing-room. The furniture had been good, but the room looked neglected—a shabby carpet was threadbare, and there was no fire in the grate.

The housekeeper had given her no idea where she might find the dining-room, so she opened one or two doors to find a small sitting-room, a storeroom and a cupboard, before she discovered the dining-room.

There was a huge oval-shaped table in the centre. At the far end was a sideboard, on which stood a silver galleon and two silver candlesticks—all, she noticed, sadly in need of a polish. Turning to the table, she saw it was laid for two and she wondered, a little anxiously, what her new charge would be like. At least she will be young, Eliza thought.

The tall windows were hung with tattered curtains. At one time there had been a pattern of fleur-de-lys, but this had long since disappeared and they were faded and worn.

Eliza drew back one of the curtains and peered out. There was no sign of any human being and no sound but the crashing of the waves over the shingle.

Eliza let the curtain drop and turned back into the room. At that moment, the door opened and a girl, about Eliza's age, stood tremulously on the threshold.

Mercy on us, she is nervous. I do believe she is a little afraid of me, Eliza thought. It was a strange feeling, for never, in all her years, had anyone been afraid of Eliza, though she herself had often been scared—of her employer, of her cousin's ill-tempered wife, of the master at the school she had attended briefly.

'Do come in,' Eliza said, her eye taking in the girl's deep jade velvet dress, the single string of pearls, and her red-gold hair. Eliza noticed that her charge was very pale with the sort of pallor that comes from being confined indoors too long.

'My name is Eliza Dunlop,' Eliza told the girl. 'And I am to be your . . .' She didn't quite know what to say. She wasn't a governess or a nursemaid. Mr Humbie had described her as 'companion', so Eliza said, 'I am to be your companion. We can go out together for walks. We could read novels together,' she said, becoming more enthusiastic.

The girl's face broke into a shy smile.

'How do you do,' she said slowly, with more than a hint of a French accent. 'My name is Catriona Stuart.'

'Well, I'm sure we shall get along very well,' Eliza said, more confidently than she felt. 'Do you sew?'

The girl nodded.

'Yes. The nuns taught me.'

'I can barely sew a seam,' Eliza said, unable to keep a note of pride out of her voice. She had resisted all attempts to teach her—there was nothing more boring than sitting sewing, she had decided early on.

'Your soup's ready.' The old housekeeper opened the door. Eliza, from force of habit, rushed to help her. But the woman brushed her away. 'I can manage on my own,' she said brusquely, laying a plate of soup at each place and a rough oatmeal loaf in the centre of the table.

'I am hungry after my journey,' Eliza said as the door closed behind the housekeeper. She passed the wooden platter of bread to the girl, who shook her head.

With a sigh, Eliza picked up her spoon. Surely, she thought, things would look a good deal better after a meal.

The broth was at least hot—Eliza was grateful for that. She broke off a piece of the loaf and offered it to the girl, who again shook her head.

'I am not hungry,' she said, laying down her spoon.

'You must eat,' Eliza told her firmly.

Reluctantly, the girl swallowed a mouthful or two of the soup. But all through the meal she was silent.

Afterwards, Eliza, with a sinking heart, said,

'Shall we sit in the drawing-room?'

The girl nodded and led the way upstairs. Even though the room was lacking in comfort, the large windows looked out on to the bay and far away there was the Bass Rock and the shores beyond.

This is better, Eliza thought, looking out of the window. At least tomorrow she would be able to watch the fishing boats in the bay. Now a few passers-by, huddled in greatcoats and shawls, made their way along the narrow path. And beyond that was the shore. What lay at the end of the shore, Eliza wondered. Well, there would be time to explore in the days ahead, but at least, she thought, there was some life outside this gaunt, depressing house.

'What do you like to do?'

'I am quite content,' the girl said.

'Then perhaps we might have a game of cards.'

The girl hesitated.

'I do not know how to play.'

'I'll teach you. We'll begin tomorrow.'

Catriona did not seem very enthusiastic.

'And do you read? Novels? The works of Sir Walter Scott, maybe?' Eliza asked a little desperately. Her work as companion was going to be hard, she could see that.

'A little.' The girl paused. 'I do not read much English.'

Ah, so that was the answer. That was at least something she could do.

21

'Then I will teach you,' Eliza said cheerfully. 'So what would you like to do tomorrow?'

'I would like,' Catriona said slowly, 'perhaps to walk by the sea. And maybe to look at the shop windows.'

'Well,' Eliza replied, 'tomorrow we will go out and see the shops.' She was doubtful whether there would be any shops at all in this benighted place, let alone one displaying the latest fashions from London. But, she told herself, at least there was some show of interest.

The girl's jade green velvet dress was plain but well cut, and the lace she wore at her neck was delicately worked—probably by the nuns, Eliza thought.

'Then tomorrow we will go out walking,' she promised.

As she carried her candle upstairs to the plainly furnished room, she thought, this is going to be hard. Perhaps even harder than working for old Miss Gregory. But she decided that there was no use in being downhearted.

Before going to bed, she pulled back the curtains—they also were thin and shabby, like the curtains downstairs, and the lining was in tatters.

Outside, she could still see the lights of the boats on the Firth. And she wished that she could step on board one of the boats, and sail away to the Low Countries, forgetting for a moment how rough the sea had been on the short trip from Leith. She remembered being told that the ships from the Fife harbours took coal and potatoes to the Dutch ports, and brought back as ballast the brick-red tiles that were used on the roofs of houses along the coast.

Dreamily, she gazed out of the window, imagining these distant ports. Then suddenly out of the corner of her eye, she could see a figure in a black cloak walking slowly along the shore. He—it must be a man, she decided— walked then paused, and walked again. Then, as if making up his mind, he turned round and looked up at the windows of Shore House.

Eliza knew that he could not possibly see her, but she shrank back all the same.

She could not see his face clearly, but his movements seemed purposeful. He was not, she decided, simply out for an evening stroll. So what was he doing here? And why did he keep looking up at the house?

She waited, wondering if he was a visitor— in which case, why did he not ring the bell? But there was no sound from the front of the house. He stood very still, as if he was waiting for something. A signal, perhaps?

Then he glanced around, as if to make sure he was not being observed and, very swiftly, he slipped down the narrow alley between the houses. Eliza tried to see where he had gone, but it was impossible. She waited for a moment or two—perhaps he would reappear. But there was no sign.

Deeply puzzled, she closed the curtains. She hunched her shoulders and rubbed her hands together against the damp chill, but she knew it wasn't the atmosphere in the room that made her shiver.

All evening, she had fought the strange feeling of unease that seemed to grip her. But now she knew there was something very sinister about this house. That housekeeper was more like a jailer, Eliza thought. And. then she felt as if a hand had gripped her wrist. Was that what Mistress Kilbain was—a jailer? But, she told herself briskly, she was being ridiculous. She was imagining things.

Perhaps, she thought as she slipped between the icy sheets, and blew out her candle, perhaps it will all look very much better in the morning.

But who was this mysterious stranger?

NEW FRIENDS

The next morning was more promising. As soon as the breakfast table had been cleared, Eliza said to her charge, 'Would you like to go out? You said you would like to look at the sea, and perhaps the shops. Not that there are many shops in Kingsferry.' She was fairly certain of that.

The girl's face brightened.

'Yes, perhaps.'

'It's a fine morning,' Eliza said briskly. The storm of the previous evening had gone, and sunlight warmed the red pantiled roofs.

Perhaps, Eliza thought, she will find something to talk about.

Catriona had been silent all during breakfast, so Eliza had tried to find out where she had come from, and why she had come to this bleak house in Fife, with Mistress Kilbain as wardress. And what was she, Eliza, doing here?

She gave up—there was time to find out. Meantime, it was too good a morning to waste.

'If you will fetch your cloak,' she told Catriona, 'then we can set off.'

Her cloak, Eliza noticed, was of a fine blue velvet, with a hood. The cloak's hood was trimmed with dark blue matching braid, fastened by a silver clasp. How different from mine, Eliza thought, wrapping her shabby black woollen cloak around her.

In fact, she thought, though we are the same height, we are very different. She admitted to herself that Catriona was beautiful, with her delicate pearly complexion, her heart-shaped face, her red-gold hair, and soft brown eyes. Whereas she was plain—she seldom had time to look in a mirror, but she knew that her face, sprinkled with freckles, and her tilted nose were not made for beauty. Her hair, too, was

25

a nondescript light brown colour. But there was nothing she could do about it, and it was not likely that any young man would ever want to court her—certainly not for her looks, she thought.

However, for now she had other things to think about. She led the way downstairs.

We will walk along the front, she decided. Perhaps we could look at the fishing boats—though some of them will be away at sea.

She unlatched the front door and pushed it open, enjoying the fresh salt smell that seemed to sweep into the damp hallway of the old house.

'And where might you be going?'

Mistress Kilbain appeared suddenly. Neither of the girls had noticed her coming silently out from the kitchen premises.

'Just for a short walk to take the air this fine morning.'

'That you will not. There was no talk of walks and taking the air.' She glared at Eliza.

'And why not?' Eliza was determined to stand up to the housekeeper. 'I am to look after Miss Catriona, and she will take no harm from a little fresh air. Indeed,' she went on, 'you can see for yourself how pale she is. It is not good for her to be cooped up indoors.'

'These were not my orders,' the housekeeper muttered.

'Orders from whom, pray?' Eliza asked.

The housekeeper glared at her and turned

away.

It was a bright morning, with a fresh breeze coming off the sea, and today the sunlight sparkled on the waves. Eliza's spirits rose.

She had to admit there was little to see along the front—though Catriona peered with interest into the shoemaker's window, and sniffed appreciatively as they passed the baker's shop.

After about half an hour, Eliza suggested they walk down to the harbour and watch the fishermen working on their boats. She liked the names of the boats—there was the *Pimpernel,* the *Good Hope,* the *Sarah Ann.* Suddenly she noticed a small, rather familiar figure running along the quay.

'Good morning—it's Robbie, isn't it?' She smiled at the boy. 'You helped me with my valise yesterday evening.'

He gazed up at her, a grubby, impudent boy, but Eliza felt a warmth about the morning. He was the first person she had met in this bleak little town, and he had been cheerful and obliging. Suddenly she didn't feel quite so alone and friendless.

'This is Robbie,' she told Catriona. 'He helped to carry my bag.' Catriona said nothing and Eliza felt a little exasperated.

'Why are you not at school?' she asked the boy.

'Me?' He looked astonished at her question. 'I don't go to the school. I run messages for folk.'

'Robbie!' one of the fishermen called out.

'We'd better not keep you from your work,' Eliza said with a smile as he dashed off.

'Time to go back, I think,' Eliza said to her companion, though she would have liked to stay and watch the fishermen setting off from the harbour.

They were making their way slowly up the road from the harbour when a girl about Eliza's age, came racing down. Unable to stop herself she cannoned into Catriona, then regained her balance, with a flood of apologies.

'You must excuse my sister,' the young man who had followed her at a more sober pace said. 'She runs everywhere. She will never make a lady.'

He swept off his hat and gave a slight bow towards Catriona and Eliza.

'I hope you are not hurt,' he said to Catriona.

She shook her head.

'No. I thank you.'

'I'm so sorry,' the girl said. 'Jamie's quite right. I should try to behave more like a lady. But I always run down this hill.' She smiled. She had, Eliza noted, a cheerful, engaging expression. She did not wear a bonnet or a cap, and her fair hair hung in ringlets with curls over her forehead. Her dress was plain, without frills or furbelows at the hem, and although she looked neat and tidy, Eliza, who had observed the fashionable ladies walking along George Street, felt it was some time since the girl's outfit had been in the height of fashion.

'May we introduce ourselves?' the girl went on. 'I don't think we've met before. I am Maggie Grieve, and this is my brother, Jamie, and our father is the minister here.'

'I am Eliza Dunlop.' Eliza smiled. 'And this is Miss Catriona Stuart.'

'Our pleasure,' Maggie said, and her brother bowed. Eliza glanced at him. He was of medium height, sandy-haired, with a frank, open expression.

'I don't think I have seen you in the streets,' Maggie observed. 'Are you new here?'

'I have just arrived,' Eliza explained. 'And Miss Catriona, too. We are staying at Shore House.'

There was a sudden silence, and Eliza caught brother and sister exchanging a glance.

'Oh,' Maggie said. 'So . . .' she floundered a little, 'you are new to Kingsferry. I hope,' she said, recovering herself, 'I hope you will come and visit us at the manse. We are always at home. At least I am. My brother is a lawyer in Edinburgh, but is here for a little recovering from a fever.'

'I hope you are better, sir,' Eliza said to Jamie.

'Thank you, I'm almost completely

recovered.' He smiled down at her, and Eliza thought how pleasant he looked. Not handsome, not like the man in her dreams, but with a tanned face and a ready smile. Eliza had met very few young men, and it was pleasant to find how ordinary Maggie's brother was, and how easy to talk to.

'Yes, do come and see us. We will arrange a day.'

'And now we must go back,' Eliza remembered.

Jamie bowed again as they turned away.

'Well!' Eliza said as they reached the door of Shore House. 'We have only just arrived and already we have made three friends: Master Jamie and Miss Maggie, and that rascal of a boy at the harbour. That is good for one morning, is it not?'

Catriona was still rather silent, but this could not dampen Eliza's spirits. She felt that probably the girl was only shy, and was wary of being too frank with someone she did not know. Probably in time, she would be more forthcoming—look at the pleasant, though shy way she had smiled at Maggie and her brother.

That night, as Eliza drew the curtains, she remembered with pleasure the day's meetings. But something nagged at her memories of the day. Then she recalled. It was the silence when she had mentioned Shore House, and the swift glance between brother and sister.

There was something very strange about

Shore House. Why did local people not want to speak of it?

AN INVITATION

During the next few days Eliza tried to get to know her charge. Although Catriona did not speak much, she was agreeable. Now and then her features would break into a sweet smile and Eliza decided that she could be a pleasant companion, if she ever came to know her.

And her clothes! She did not have many, but they were all fairly new and expertly made. There was that blue velvet cloak with a hood, for example.

Catriona's day dresses were of simple wool, but the kerchiefs she wore were exquisite, of finely worked lace. And her boots were of the finest leather.

'The nuns taught me to sew,' Catriona explained, when she caught Eliza admiring a lace collar.

'What fine work!' Eliza murmured. At the same time, she wanted to know more about this convent—where was it, how had Catriona come there, and why had she left? But it was hard to have a conversation—she had no French, and Catriona's English was rather limited.

'I have an idea,' she announced one day, as

they finished the bowls of barley broth that the housekeeper had set before them. 'I will try to teach you some more English—and you will teach me to sew.'

'I would like that,' Catriona said with that slow gentle smile. 'When shall we begin?'

'Today,' Eliza said. 'I think,' she reflected, 'that I will have the easier time. I have never learned to sew a seam. Oh, how often I have pricked my finger with a needle and bled over a delicate piece of stitching.'

Catriona did not appear to understand this, so she said no more. But afterwards, when they were seated by the window upstairs, Eliza produced a chapbook she'd had as a small child.

'Can you read this?' she asked, pointing to the word.

Catriona had obviously learned some English and she repeated the words obligingly. It would be good, Eliza thought, if Catriona learned about the food they ate.

'Bannocks,' she explained. 'Kail. Scotch broth.' Catriona did not eat a great deal, and showed little interest in learning about food. What else could she try, Eliza thought a little desperately.

Perhaps, she decided, Catriona would enjoy hearing some of the novels of Sir Walter Scott. Maybe, when they went to the manse, she might borrow some of Sir Walter's tales. There was, for example, 'Ivanhoe', which she had enjoyed, or 'The Heart Of Midlothian'. Her spirits rose at the thought of reading aloud to Catriona. It was far better than reading religious tracts to Miss Gregory, who had disapproved of novels, and Eliza had been obliged to read her own books late at night, by the light of a single candle.

The sewing lessons were not going well. Eliza progressed from sewing a plain seam to mending the hem of her only dress. Catriona was a patient teacher. Far better than I will ever be, Eliza thought ruefully, as Catriona only smiled and cheerfully unpicked a faulty seam, or kindly bound up a finger that Eliza had pricked with a needle.

But, oh, the days passed slowly. It was very quiet in Kingsferry, she decided. Sometimes there was a little excitement when the mail coach arrived, and drew up at the inn, before continuing its journey along the turnpike road to St Andrews. Or when a two-wheeled carriage, drawn by two grey horses, drew up and there was a flurry of activity as the ostlers hurried to tend to the horses.

Eliza wished that she could meet with the brother and sister from the manse. She had not met many young people and had enjoyed the friendly banter between the two.

She realised she had very little idea of how people should behave in society. All she had learned from her years with the difficult old lady was how to read from the Bible and religious tracts and pour out claret. And even though she had read as well as the works of Sir Walter Scott, several romantic novels, which she had bought from her hard-earned wages, she knew, realistically, that people did not behave in this little town as they did in high society.

So she was surprised when, one day, the bell jangled at the big front door. It seemed that no-one ever rang the bell. Tradesmen came down the alley to the kitchen door, and the fishwives would not call, but sing out in the street, 'Fine fresh herring!'

She was about to run downstairs when she heard the housekeeper come out of the kitchen, and turn the key, which was rather stiff as the door was so seldom opened.

There on the doorstep, in an old wool dress, really too warm for the fine summer morning, stood Maggie, the minister's daughter. She stood, smiling, as if she was perfectly sure of a warm welcome.

'You must be Mistress Kilbain,' she greeted the housekeeper, who eyed her suspiciously. 'And I am Maggie Grieve, daughter of the Reverend Joshua Grieve.'

Eliza, a few steps behind the housekeeper, cried out, 'Why, it is good to see you! Please come in.'

But the housekeeper barred the way, and although Maggie peered into the recesses of the hall, she was not to be allowed over the

34

threshold

However, Maggie was undeterred.

'I have come with an invitation,' she said cheerfully. 'Here we do not leave calling cards, as they do in the city, so I thought I would come in person. My father would like to meet you, Miss Eliza, and Miss Stuart, and I would like you to come and drink a dish of tea with us. Shall we say next Thursday at about three o'clock?'

'Thank you. We will be delighted to accept,' Eliza said.

The housekeeper intervened.

'No, miss, the young lady will not be going out. She is in my care. And Miss Dunlop is here to look after her, so she will not be accepting invitations to tea parties.'

'Oh, it's not a tea party,' Maggie insisted, undeterred. 'We are very plain folk, and most respectable, I do assure you. As my father is a minister, of course we would be—respectable, I mean. And I'm sure Miss Catriona would enjoy the stroll and seeing the garden.'

'Oh yes, she would,' Eliza said swiftly. 'Thank you kindly, Miss Grieve. We shall be happy to accept.'

The housekeeper looked for a moment as if she were about to protest, but then she thought better of it, and with a shrug of her shoulders, turned and made her way back to the kitchen.

'My, she is fierce, is she not?' Maggie

whispered. 'I should be terrified of her.'

'Won't you come in?' Eliza asked 'I had just been thinking of you and your brother.'

'Kindly, I hope,' Maggie said with that pleasant frankness. 'If you come to visit us you will see that I can behave with more propriety than I showed the other day, when I nearly knocked over poor Miss Stuart. I had better not come in. Though,' she went on, 'I would dearly love to see inside this house. But your housekeeper would probably not let me out again.' She gave that unaffected, merry laugh and Eliza now felt more cheerful.

'I look forward greatly to the visit,' Eliza said.

'And I.' Maggie waved at a passing group of children. 'The manse is at the top of the hill. My father is looking forward to meeting you. My brother, too, of course. Though you have already met. Oh, dear me, how I do run on!'

As she closed the door, Eliza felt herself smile. How much brighter life was going to be!

A MIDNIGHT VISITOR

During the next few days Eliza became accustomed to the routine of Shore House. How different it was from the daily pattern of life in the grand house in Heriot Row.

After a little she no longer found it strange

36

to wake to the sound of the waves crashing over the shingle and the cry of the seagulls, instead of the clip-clop of horses' hooves and the loud voices of the men who brought the milk in churns.

But one night, she found it hard to fall asleep. She kept turning over in her mind the questions about the house and its strange occupants. Who was Catriona? She was pleasant enough, good natured, but quiet and gave no information about herself apart from the fact that she had grown up in the convent. And who was the strange housekeeper? Who owned the house? And why were the local people silent when it was mentioned? She remembered the glances that had been exchanged between Maggie and Jamie.

At last, deciding that she could not sleep, she decided to go down to the kitchen in search of some buttermilk and maybe a bannock left over from supper. She took her candle and, shivering a little, wrapped her shawl around her. It was, she guessed, a little after midnight.

On the way downstairs, she peeped in at Catriona's door, but the girl was asleep, and she closed the door very softly.

As she reached the ground floor of the house, Eliza stopped in astonishment. It couldn't be voices coming from the kitchen at this time of night, could it? Since coming to Shore House, Eliza had never seen anyone visiting, and certainly not at midnight.

She hesitated. Why not, she asked herself. I have every right to go into the kitchen to find a drink and a piece to eat. She grasped the candle firmly, and made her way very softly along the passage to the kitchen quarters. She paused outside the door. There were two voices—one that of the housekeeper, the other a man's voice, argumentative.

Not wanting to be seen, Eliza blew out her candle, and inched a little closer to the door.

The man's voice grew louder.

'I've told ye afore, there's to be nae fowk comin'in.'

'I've done ma best.' The housekeeper's tone was sulky. 'An' what wad ye hae done? They'll be safe gaun tae the manse. The minister's an auld man. I canna keep her a prisoner for ever,' she went on.

'That's what ye were telt.' The man thumped his fist on the table and Eliza could hear the pots clattering. 'I've got my orders, missus. She's to be kept safe here, until . . .'

Eliza, leaning forward, could not hear the next bit, but in her eagerness to listen to the conversation, she knocked against a coal scuttle.

'What's that?'

Eliza shrank back into the shadows as the man leapt to his feet.

'It's naething. There's naebody in the house but thae lassies, and they're both in their beds,'

Mistress Kilbain reassured him. 'It'll be the cat, chasing a mouse.'

'Ah, well.' The man sat down again. 'Here, fill that up.' Eliza could hear him thumping his tankard on the table. 'I've a thirst on me.'

It was not safe to remain longer.

'And hoo's the lass frae Edinburgh?' Eliza could hear his rasping tones.

'She'll gie nae trouble.'

Eliza shivered when she heard this. Until now she had not been afraid, but the housekeeper's steely reply made her suddenly realise that she was in danger. An orphan, with no friends, no family—now she knew why she had been chosen for the post. Who would care if she disappeared?

She decided to go back to bed, where she could think over all that she had heard and decide what was best to do. But before she went, she moved as stealthily as she could towards the door, which was open only a few inches, and looked into the room.

The housekeeper was sitting upright at the table, looking directly at the man who lolled in his chair opposite her, his feet on the table, the tankard in his hand. He was dark, with a swarthy complexion and, Eliza guessed, of medium height. Where had she seen him before?

Turning swiftly, Eliza inched her way along the passage. Without a candle, it was too dark to see where she was going, so she

39

let her fingers follow the rough plaster of the wall until she reached the hall. To her relief, the couple in the kitchen had not heard her movements. Slowly, her heart beating wildly, she made her way up the stairs to the first landing, then up again to her bedroom under the eaves.

With a great surge of thankfulness, she flung herself into bed, pulling the covers over her head.

She knew, her mind whirling round with unanswered questions, that there was to be little sleep that night. Exhausted and bewildered, she lay until the first slivers of light came through the thin curtains.

Wrapped in her shawl, she crept out of the bed and sat by the window, gazing out over the sea. Beyond the narrow strip of the lane the shingle beach was empty, with no sign of any human being.

But now, Eliza was sure she knew exactly where she had seen the strange midnight visitor to the kitchen.

It was the man she had glimpsed on the shore—the stranger in a dark cloak, the man she had seen that first night who had gazed with such intensity at the windows of Shore House.

SMUGGLERS

Liza fell asleep at last, but she woke heavy-eyed as she recalled the events of the night before. However, she consoled herself as she climbed out of bed, it was a bright morning and today she and Catriona were going to visit the manse in the afternoon.

Her spirits rose. There was a way out of this situation, she told herself. And now she had new friends, and she was sure that, for the first time in her life, they would be real friends, the kind who would help and advise her. She realised that never before had she had anyone in whom she could confide. And Maggie was so good-natured, she thought, and would surely be a helpful and sensible friend.

So it was with a lighter heart that she went downstairs to find Catriona already at the breakfast table.

'Did you sleep well?' she asked

Catriona looked up with a smile.

'Very well, I thank you.'

'You heard nothing? No sounds in the night?'

Catriona shook her head.

'No, nothing.'

'It's a fine morning,' Eliza observed. 'Today we go to visit our new friends.'

Catriona, a little shyly in her halting

41

English, said, 'I do not know them.'

'Ah, but you will,' Eliza told her cheerfully. 'They are young—about your age, I think, and very friendly.'

Had Catriona never known any young people, Eliza wondered. Well, this was a good way to make new friends.

That afternoon both the girls dressed with care. Eliza, to be truthful, had nothing to wear that was suitable for going out on a visit. But as she brushed her one wool day dress, she remembered that Maggie would hardly be dressed in the height of fashion.

Catriona, on the other hand, had put on a dress of fine grey wool, the neckline decorated with small pearls, the skirt just skimming her ankles to show a fine pair of soft leather boots. She carried a reticule of grey silk, and wore the midnight blue cloak that Eliza had admired, with a bonnet trimmed with soft grey feathers. She carried a small swansdown muff, and wore a gold chain as her only jewellery. She looked like a young lady of fashion—rather like the young ladies that Eliza had seen promenading along George Street back in Edinburgh.

Out of doors, Eliza breathed in the fresh air, there was a pleasant light breeze, and the view over the Forth was clear.

'There in the distance,' she explained to Catriona, 'you can almost see as far as Leith.'

The manse stood high on the hill above the village, a large stone-built house with a path

42

winding to the front door. It looked imposing, Eliza thought, a house suitable for a minister. For a moment she had qualms about their visit. Would they really be welcome, or had Maggie simply acted on impulse? But she led Catriona up the path, and rang the bell at the front door.

'Here you are!' Maggie flung open the door. 'I have so looked forward to seeing you.'

Eliza noticed immediately that Maggie's hair sprung wildly from her head as if it had not been dressed or combed since she rose that morning, and she still wore a drugget apron over her dress.

'Oh, do excuse me,' she said, tugging at the apron. 'I have been in the kitchen. We have a maid, Isla, and she has been given the afternoon off. So I am cook today!' She laughed. 'I am so pleased to have guests. Isla has already made a honey cake and I made a seed cake, and we will have rowan jelly on the scones. Now come in. You know my brother, Jamie, but you have not met my father.'

'That is easily remedied, my dear.' The tall, stooping figure that came along the passage shook his head at his daughter. 'Do not keep our young friends on the doorstep, Maggie. Come in, come in. You are most heartily welcome.' He beamed on them and shook hands with Eliza, then Catriona.

'Tea is in the parlour today,' Maggie said, throwing aside her apron and leading the way.

43

'As we have guests.'

The parlour was a small room leading off the hall, furnished with cumbersome old-fashioned furniture. Although it was a warm day, a fire burned in the grate—the grate surround itself was of blue and white Dutch tiles. Two large bookcases held an array of books, and even more books spilled on to the tables dotted around the room, It was a comfortable room, Eliza thought, not like the usual parlour.

'Please, sit down,' Maggie said, pointing to the horsehair sofa. 'I think that is quite comfortable,' she said a little doubtfully. 'Or maybe this chair.'

'My dear,' her father said, 'it is too fine a day to sit long indoors. Why do I not show our guest my garden?'

Maggie laughed.

'My father's garden is a source of great pride to him. He spends as long over his garden as he does over his sermons, I'll be bound.'

Joshua Grieve shook his head at his daughter.

'You will not believe anything that my daughter says—or at least believe very little. She exaggerates a great deal.'

'Ah, here you are!' The door burst open and Jamie appeared. 'I'm sorry I wasn't here to greet you,' he apologised. 'I was held up waiting for the courier!' He bowed over

44

Catriona's hand. 'Miss Stuart, it's a pleasure to meet you again.

'And. Miss Dunlop—you, too.' He smiled and bowed to Eliza politely.

'I was suggesting,' his father said, 'that perhaps Miss Stuart would care to see the garden. On such a fine summer's day, it is at its best, if I dare say so.'

Catriona nodded shyly.

'Yes, please.'

'Then we will walk. You will like to see my old Scottish roses—they have a most beautiful scent. They were grown from cuttings, given to me by a very old friend.'

As the door closed behind them, there was for a moment or two a rather embarrassed silence.

'What a lot of books you have!' Eliza exclaimed.

'A great many.' Maggie nodded. 'And even more in our father's study. In fact, it is hard to get in the door.'

'Indeed,' Eliza said, suddenly shy.

'But,' Jamie said briskly, 'you did not come here to talk about books—though we have a great many, as you have noticed, and you are free to borrow any that you wish.' He sat down on the horsehair sofa, and leaned forward.

'You have come here to talk to us. I think you have problems and anxieties, and perhaps we can help,' he said kindly.

'I . . .' Eliza glanced towards the door.

45

'Please don't concern yourself. My father and Miss Stuart will be a little time. He knows that you will want to talk to us and it was arranged beforehand that he should take Miss Stuart into the garden. So . . .'

Eliza felt as if a burden had been lifted from her shoulders. She had been quite right. These were friends, and she could trust them.

'Oh!' she said. 'I hardly know where to begin.'

'At the beginning. How you came here,' Jamie said, smiling at her.

She began her story, and she explained how she had glimpsed the man in the kitchen and what she had overheard the previous night.

'And you have seen him before?'

'I'm almost certain,' Eliza said firmly, 'that it was the man I saw in the lawyer's office. Mr Humbie is the lawyer's name.'

Jamie drew in his breath sharply

'I have heard of him,' he said a little grimly. 'As you know, I am a lawyer—albeit a humble one—in Edinburgh, but I've heard tell of this man. I will write to my friend in Edinburgh and ask him to make enquiries. Very discreetly you understand.'

'And what about the house?' Eliza was puzzled. 'The first time we met, I divined there was something strange about the house, something that people did not want to talk about.'

Jamie nodded.

'No-one knows about the owner. There is that strange old housekeeper, and people come and go.'

'People say it is haunted,' Maggie put in.

'Oh, nonsense!' her brother admonished her sharply. 'You will frighten Miss Dunlop, and it seems to me she has had quite enough to frighten her already.'

'I have heard of a ghost,' Maggie continued stubbornly 'And there was the Black Lady that people still speak of. Remember, she was said to haunt that old house by the burn. People were afraid to go anywhere near the house. It was said that even the sight of her drove folks mad.'

'That's nonsense.' Jamie laughed. 'The owner—I forget his name—made her up. He meant to scare people away from the house which he used to store smuggled wines and spirits. There was no such ghost.'

'I could cope quite happily with a ghost,' Eliza reassured Maggie. 'I am not afraid of ghosts. I think there are probably lots of ghostly figures flitting around the streets of Edinburgh.'

'I don't think you are frightened of very many things, Miss Dunlop,' Jamie said, again with that frank, open smile.

She hesitated.

'There is another thing,' she said. 'I have seen boats come and go to the harbour at night when it is dark. Oh, I know it is long light these

47

summer evenings, but I am surprised that they are out in the bay in the middle of the night. And there are no lights on the boats.'

'Ah.' Jamie nodded. 'That will be the smugglers.'

'Smugglers?' Eliza's voice rose.

'They come from the Netherlands,' Jamie explained, 'to ports all along the Fife coast, like Anstruther, Crail, and other fishing villages. Small craft go out to the boats and bring back the casks of brandy and gin. It seems strange to me that the smugglers are so seldom caught, for many people know about them. They'll bring the casks on handcarts or strong men may carry them, and they'll be hidden in houses and cellars. And, on the Isle of May, there are caves which are used as storage for wines and tobacco.'

'So,' Eliza said thoughtfully, 'Shore House may be a safe place for smugglers?'

'I would not be surprised,' Jamie agreed.

'Still,' he went on, 'I think there is more going on in Shore House than simply hiding contraband.'

'But,' Eliza said thoughtfully, 'I am worried about Catriona. I know nothing about her—where she came from, and why she is being held like a prisoner.'

'I will make enquiries,' Jamie promised. 'And when I return to Edinburgh as soon as there is news, I will get word to you. We have a messenger who can safely bring you word.'

'A messenger?'

'You have met Robbie.' He smiled. 'He's a wild lad, but an honest one.'

'And bright and quick,' Maggie put in. 'I wish he would stick to his books. Our father has tried to teach him his letters, but had no success, I'm afraid.'

'And another problem,' Eliza said. 'I find it a little difficult to converse with Catriona, because she speaks so little English. She was brought up in a convent and can sew beautifully, but I have tried to teach her about the food we eat—bannocks, kail, and so on, but it is hard. She knows some English that, it seems, she learned in the convent where she lived, but we are no nearer finding out who she is, how she came here, and why.'

Jamie threw back his head and laughed. Eliza thought how pleasant it would be to have a brother like him, who made light of difficulties, but yet was perfectly at ease and capable of dealing with all kinds of situations. Perhaps, she decided, it was because he was a lawyer, and accustomed to clients and their problems.

'I can see,' he said kindly, 'that it might not be easy to get to the root of a problem with such a limited vocabulary—bannocks and so on.'

She knew he was laughing at her, but she did not find it at all offensive, and smiled back at him.

49

'I wonder,' he said thoughtfully, 'if we can solve this difficulty.' Then he added suddenly, 'I wonder, too, if it has anything to do with the King Over The Water, as they used to call the father of Bonnie Prince Charlie.'

'But surely,' Maggie protested, 'everyone has long forgotten about the Prince. After all, even King George has called himself a Jacobite. I heard my father read something of the sort from the Scotsman. No-one thinks of them as enemies any more.'

'True,' her brother said slowly, 'but there are still staunch Jacobite families around. In Crail there is one such family.'

At that moment they heard voices. The minister's, deep and slow, and surprisingly, Catriona's voice, high and sweet.

'Here we are,' Joshua Grieve said. 'Our guest has never seen such fine roses, or at least she was kind enough to say so. We have had a most agreeable tour of the garden.'

He beamed, rather vaguely, on the company. Catriona, too, was smiling at her host.

'And she has been telling me something of her life,' he explained. 'Such fine people, those nuns who taught her.'

'But how . . . ?' Eliza was at a loss. Catriona had such limited English, or had she been hiding her knowledge of the language? Surely she would not be so devious.

The minister looked amused at her

50

bewilderment.

'I admit that I am not widely versed in languages,' he said. 'Hebrew, yes, some knowledge of the tongues of the Middle East, and,' he paused, 'I spent some time studying in Switzerland as a young man, so I learned the language there.' He turned to Catriona. 'Miss Stuart and I had a most agreeable conversation. In French, of course.'

THE RIGHTFUL HEIR

'So . . .' The minister looked round the gathering, then spoke in careful French to Catriona, who nodded and smiled.

'Miss Stuart does not object to my telling you of what we have spoken,' he said.

Eliza leaned forward eagerly.

'Firstly,' he began, and Eliza stifled a groan of impatience. Surely this good and kindly man was not about to begin a sermon. 'Firstly, my friends,' he continued, 'I have established that Miss Stuart was born in France, and was educated by nuns at a convent in Belgium. She thought that she was an orphan of no particular descent.'

Like me, Eliza thought.

'But a year ago, two unknown men came to visit the convent and obtained permission to speak to her. To Miss Stuart's surprise,

51

she was told that she was of distinguished lineage. It had been established by a small group of Jacobites on the continent, that she was the great-granddaughter of Prince Charles Edward—Bonnie Prince Charlie,' he added helpfully, with a nod towards Eliza. 'By his lawful wife, he had a son who lived only a year and, so it is believed, daughters. And the Jacobites believe Miss Stuart here may well be the descendant of one of the daughters.'

'Well!' Eliza was almost speechless. Catriona sat, her hands folded demurely in her lap, clearly not too disturbed by the way he had revealed the secret.

'I don't understand,' Maggie said. 'After all this time,' she said with a nod to Catriona, 'why are they anxious to bring her to Scotland?'

'Ah,' the minister said. 'There had been much careful and devious planning.'

'But,' Jamie put in, 'I understood there was a grandson—an illegitimate grandson—who's still alive? Has he no claim at all? Is he not considered as a claimant to the throne?'

'His name is also Charles Edward,' the minister replied, who already knew a great deal about the Stuarts. 'He has no interest in politics, and no desire to be involved in any plot. It is my understanding that the plotters know of him and believe that he does not present any danger to their cause.'

'Surely,' Jamie added, 'there must be other descendants who have a greater claim than

Miss Stuart here?'

'Not that we know of,' his father said. 'But there are always fanatics eager to prove that there is a descendant entitled to be the rightful King or Queen of Scotland, and what better time to launch a coup against King George the Fourth, than on his visit to Scotland?'

'Why did she not tell us?' Eliza asked. 'Why is she here?'

The minister held up his hand as if stilling an unruly mob.

'All in good time,' he said. 'Secondly, these men told her that she was to come to Scotland and she would be brought here by boat in the next few months. They told the Mother Superior of Miss Stuart's history, and that the King would be willing to receive her. After all, we know that he has shown an interest in all things pertaining to the Jacobites.

'It seems, though. I am not sure why, that the good Mother Superior agreed to this, and in due course, Miss Stuart was taken, in the care of an elderly nun, to the port of Antwerp. She was given a whole new wardrobe of fine clothes—much finer than anything she had worn in the convent. There was jewellery, too—a fine gold chain, a locket, and other items. There she was handed into the care of a middle-aged sharp-tongued woman, who spoke in Scots, or at least in a language she could not understand.'

'That was surely Mistress Kilbain, the

housekeeper!' Eliza exclaimed.

The minister smiled at her.

'Yes, so it would appear. And she was brought to Shore House. She did not know that she was to be held more or less a prisoner.'

'But why,' Eliza burst out, 'why did she not tell me of her history? She said nothing to me.' She felt a little hurt, since she believed that she and Catriona had become good friends in the short time they had known each other.

The minister spoke again in his careful French to Catriona, who replied rapidly.

'Ah, yes,' he said. 'She was afraid to trust you,' he told Eliza. 'She did not know whether you had been brought to Shore House to act as a guard.'

Catriona spoke in English.

'I am sorry, Eliza. Now I know you are a friend. But then, I did not know.'

'Catriona,' Maggie said gently, 'did you know that you were a descendant of the Prince? I mean, when you were growing up in the convent?'

Catriona shook her head.

'I knew nothing,' she said. 'These two men arrived and talked to Reverend Mother.' She turned to the minister and spoke in French.

He nodded wisely.

'I thought as much.' He explained to the others. 'You see, these men had persuaded the Reverend Mother that Miss Stuart was the

54

rightful heir, and so it would be fitting if she were to visit Scotland at the time of the King's visit. I believe,' he added, 'this was to seal the friendship between Hanover and Stuart. The Reverend Mother is an elderly woman, I gather, and I have no doubt she was easily persuaded.' He spoke again in his slow, careful French to Catriona.

She replied, with gestures, describing the height of the men and their features.

'One of the men,' the minister translated, 'had a dark, lean face with black hair and sharp, yellowing teeth.'

'I knew it!' Jamie exclaimed triumphantly. 'The lawyer, Humbie. It was him! He planned the whole business! I see it all,' Jamie went on. 'The King, as you already know, is planning a visit to Edinburgh very soon. And on that occasion, Miss Stuart will be taken to Edinburgh and presented to His Royal Highness, who, I gather, has expressed a fondness for all things Jacobite. The stage is set for the rebels to overthrow the King.'

'What a great deal you have learned!' Maggie said. 'But now, what should we do?' she went on in her practical fashion.

'It seems to me,' Jamie put in, 'that there will be some action as soon as the King arrives, if not before. I understand that the Royal Yacht is waiting at Greenwich and he is to sail on Saturday next week.

'And I would expect that the conspirators—

for that is what they are—would want to take Miss Stuart to Edinburgh to be there when he arrives in the city. And it is all now becoming clear,' he went on. 'I think they have kept their plans secret. It was important that Miss Stuart should be kept at a safe distance, and under guard, until the time when she was brought to Edinburgh, the King was overthrown, and she was installed as the rightful Queen of Scotland. Else why would they want to hide Miss Stuart, and why all the secrecy about Shore House?'

'There is mischief afoot,' his father agreed solemnly.

'That's all very well!' Maggie cried. 'But here is poor Catriona being kept almost a prisoner, and we are doing nothing at all to save her!'

'Be patient, my dear,' the minister said. 'We shall rush into action.'

Maggie raised her eyes to heaven and murmured, 'Rush into action, indeed! You have never rushed into action in your life, Father.'

The minister shook his head at her, but he did not seem to be offended by these comments, and Jamie chimed in.

'No, don't let us be precipitate, but be ready when speedy action is required.' He turned to Eliza. 'You know already, Miss Dunlop, that we have an obliging messenger who will bring news to you whenever necessary, day or night.'

Eliza nodded.

'I know he is about the streets early and late. And he seems to know a great deal about what is going on.'

'He is bright and quick,' Jamie said, 'though no scholar, and you may trust him absolutely. Now,' he continued, 'I would suggest that you keep a close watch on Miss Stuart. Do not let her go out of doors alone, and be aware of any strange visitors to the Shore House. At any threat of danger you must bring her right away to the manse. Is that not right?' he appealed to his sister.

'Of course,' Maggie agreed warmly. 'She will be safe here.'

The minister turned to Catriona, and explained in his slow and careful French what they had decided.

Catriona had listened to the conversation, looking from one to the other as if quite bewildered. But now her expression lightened and she smiled hesitantly.

'You are good friends,' she said.

'Indeed we are your friends,' the minister told her. 'And you may be sure I will pray for your safety, my child.'

Eliza felt as if a burden had been lifted.

'And I shall be returning to Edinburgh very soon,' Jamie said, 'so I will try to find out what schemes are planned. I am now almost certain your Mr Humbie is involved, if indeed he has not planned the whole scheme.'

'Oh!' Maggie said, clapping her hands in

delight. 'What an adventure! Oh, I know,' she added hastily, 'that there is some risk involved, but you can be sure that my brother will take good care of Catriona. It is exciting! And in this small place—why, nothing has ever happened here!'

SHOPPING TRIP

As they left, Jamie said, 'I will accompany you back to Shore House, if you will allow me.'

Eliza was about to protest.

'Thank you, sir, but we can well manage . . .' then her voice trailed away. She felt a little shaken by what she had just heard. Until now, she had not realised that Catriona might really be in danger.

'Thank you,' she said, as he offered his arm to Catriona.

When they reached the house, there was no sign of the housekeeper. Catriona smiled and nodded her thanks, then slipped inside.

'Wait a moment,' Jamie said urgently as Eliza was about to follow.

'I think you, too, may be in danger,' he said.

Eliza looked at him.

'Me?'

'Exactly. I think that perhaps already you know too much.'

'And I may be easily dispensed with,' Eliza

said gaily. 'An orphan without anyone to be concerned for her.'

'No,' Jamie said forcibly. 'Never think that. You have good friends here. If you are at all anxious, please turn to my sister and my father. He may seem a little remote, immersed in his books, but he has seen a great deal of the world. He would help you at any time and at any cost to himself.'

Eliza suddenly felt much happier.

'And,' Jamie added, 'even though I have to return to Edinburgh, a message may be sent to me. You are not alone,' he repeated.

He took off his hat, and bowed over her hand. What a pleasant, helpful young man he was, Eliza thought. If only he was tall, dark and handsome, well, she could quite fancy losing her heart to him.

After he had turned away, Eliza went indoors. As she went upstairs to take off her cloak, she could hear Catriona singing. She stopped to listen. Then Catriona appeared at the head of the stairs.

'Oh!'

'Don't stop singing,' Eliza told her with a smile.

Catriona shrugged

'It is nothing.'

'Did you learn it from the nuns?'

'I learned it . . .' Catriona stumbled over the words, 'a long time ago. I cannot remember where.'

Eliza asked no more, but she noticed that Catriona looked much brighter, and happier, too. The company had been pleasant and the family at the manse would become good friends.

But, she wondered, had Jamie anything to do with it? Look at the way he had squired Catriona down the hill. Remember how eagerly he had jumped up to press on her another piece of honey cake. Remember, too, how he had sat by her side, trying to make her smile.

No wonder Catriona was happier. Love made people happier, Eliza knew, though she herself had never been in love. But Catriona and Jamie had met only a couple of times.

Still, she understood, love could strike like lightning. You read about it in novels. Perhaps it had been that way for Jamie and Catriona. She sighed, wondering if she herself would ever fall in love.

Then she gave herself a little shake. This was no time for romantic daydreams. There was danger in the dark and gloomy Shore House—hadn't Jamie said so? So she must be alert, she decided, and look out for any odd happenings or strange people around.

*   *   *

Next morning, Catriona was a great deal brighter than she had been for a few days.

The visit to the manse has done her good, Eliza thought.

'Today,' Catriona said over breakfast, 'we go to look at the shops.'

'Very well.' Eliza finished her plate of porridge. Strange, mysterious and sharp-tongued, the housekeeper might be, but she did make very good porridge.

'And maybe,' Catriona went on, 'maybe we see our friends again.'

'Maybe,' Eliza agreed. It would be very pleasant, she thought, to see Jamie again, to glimpse that cheerful smile of his, to see the way he threw his head back when he laughed.

Oh, stop it, she told herself firmly. She was behaving like a foolish schoolgirl. Jamie was a helpful friend and that was all.

Outside, small white clouds were scudding across the sky, and it promised to be another warm day.

Before they left the house, Eliza told the housekeeper, 'We are going for a little walk. Are there any commissions I can do for you?'

She smiled as she said it, and tried to look as pleasant and helpful as she could.

But it was no use. Mistress Kilbain turned from the fire, a kettle in her hand.

'No, there's naething.'

'Vegetables, perhaps, or bread?'

'I've said there's naething, and you'll oblige me by no interfering in the household.' She glared at Eliza. 'As if it weren't bad enough, you taking the lass here, there and everywhere.'

'But why not?' Eliza was determined to stand her ground. 'I am Miss Stuart's companion—that is why I was employed—and if she wishes to go out and take the air, then why should she not?'

'Because she's no weel,' the housekeeper said.

'Oh, fiddle-de dee,' Eliza said. 'She is perfectly well. You can see for yourself that she is now eating quite well, and has a much better colour. Whatever ailed her must have been nothing at all. For you can see quite plainly she is completely recovered.'

The housekeeper's face flushed and she almost spat out her words.

'She's no supposed to go out,' she hissed at Eliza. 'That's what I was tell—' she broke off, as if she was afraid she had said too much.

'Who told you that?' Eliza tried to speak calmly, as if the housekeeper's answer was of no consequence. 'Indeed, who told you she must be kept like a prisoner?'

The housekeeper glared at her, but Eliza was determined to stand her ground.

'If you know what's good for you, my lady, you'd better no' ask questions. You do your job and I'll do mine and that'll suit the both of us. And now, I'll be glad if you'll get out of my kitchen.'

'Very well.' Eliza tried to sound cool and

62

very calm, though in fact her heart seemed to be beating wildly. She turned to go.

But the housekeeper had not finished.

'You tak tent o' what I've said,' she called after Eliza. 'I'm warnin' you.'

Eliza closed the door behind her as quietly as she could and leaned against the wall, trying to compose herself. What had the woman meant by her threat?

Then, she decided, she would try to avoid confronting the housekeeper. And wouldn't it be safer for Catriona to be out of this house, even walking to the harbour?

'Are you ready?' she called. 'Then let's be on our way.'

Eliza drew a deep breath as they walked along the lane towards the main street. She would really have preferred to be on her own, to think over what the minister had told them, and to decide in her own mind what she should do.

Wait and watch carefully, she decided, and be aware of anything unusual, as Jamie had counselled her.

But there was little time for thought. Catriona, in her elegant soft grey leather boots, was tripping happily along the road.

'I like to see the harbour and perhaps look at the shops,' she said. 'There were no shops near the convent, and I did not often go out.'

Eliza sighed. There was not a great choice of shops in the village; the shoemaker, the handloom weaver, the ironmonger. She remembered how she had enjoyed the rare occasions when she had been able to stroll along George Street in Edinburgh and admire the shop windows.

'Feegh!' Catriona wrinkled her nose as they passed the tannery.

'It's a tannery,' Eliza explained. 'Where they make the leather for shoes.' She did not feel able to explain how the process worked, so she grasped Catriona by the arm and they hurried on.

Catriona dawdled along the main street, pausing to watch the shoemaker at work outside his shop. She sniffed appreciatively at the smell of new bread from the baker's, and lifted her skirts delicately as they passed the flesher's, where offal had been flung into the gutters.

'Oh, look!' She stopped in front of a shop window. Above it was a sign, *Draper's, supplier to the gentry*. Eliza felt a little cheered. At least there was one quality shop in the village. She peered into the window until Catriona tugged at her arm.

'We go inside?'

'Very well.' Eliza nodded, and the two girls entered the small, dark, rather cramped interior, where a very elderly woman was seated behind the counter. It did not look very promising, Eliza thought, but perhaps Catriona would find something to buy.

'Ladies!' The old woman rose to her feet.

'Oh, please, sit down!' Eliza felt this elderly shopkeeper was rather too frail to be selling goods in a draper's. Surely she should be sitting before the fire, telling stories to the grandchildren around her knee.

'And what can I do for you?' the woman wheezed.

Eliza looked round. She had a little money in her reticule, but she was unsure how much anything might cost here. Though she would dearly have loved a length of silk to make a new gown, she knew that was quite out of the question. And where would she wear a silk gown in any case?

'You are visitors, are ye no'?' the old woman probed. 'Then you'll be wanting something to take home with you—a fine minding of your stay.'

Eliza hesitated. She had met few enough people in the village, and here was a chance to find out why people were afraid of the rather sinister Shore House. It couldn't simply be that it might be haunted, as Maggie had said. There must be more to it than that.

But she didn't want Catriona to hear her questioning the old woman.

'Have you . . .' she looked round wildly, 'have you ribbons?'

'Aye, that I have. You'll not find finer ribbon if you were to go to London town itself. Just you ask anybody around here and they'll tell you, Mistress Mackay has a grand stock of ribbons.'

'Yes, well.' Eliza looked around the shop. 'Can you please show me some?'

The old woman hirpled over to a chest of drawers and blew the dust off the top.

'Ribbons, ribbons,' she muttered to herself. 'Fine ribbons for fine ladies.'

With an effort she pulled the drawer open and delved with her claw-like hands into the depths of the drawer.

She spread the ribbons out on the counter.

'There you are. Take your time, ladies. You'll not find any finer.'

'I find ribbon to trim my bonnet,' Catriona said. 'Blue ribbon.'

Seeing that her friend was occupied, Eliza turned to the old woman.

'We are not visitors here. We are staying in Shore House.'

A strange expression, half fear, half curiosity, seemed to cross the old woman's features.

'Are you telling me now?'

It seemed to Eliza that she was not from Fife, with its distinctive accent. Already in the shops and the street, she could make out the accents of the villagers. But Mistress Mackay's accent reminded her of something. But what?

Then she remembered. Old Miss Gregory had had a parlour maid who came from Skye. This old woman was from the Isles, Eliza thought. And how did she come here?

'You know the house?' Eliza persisted. She saw out of the corner of her eye that Catriona was turning over the ribbons, discarding some, smoothing out others.

'Aye.' The old woman, who had been so garrulous, was suddenly withdrawn.

'I have only recently come to live there.' Eliza was determined to find out more. 'It is a very large house, is it not? And perhaps you know the housekeeper, Mistress Kilbain?'

The old woman no longer seemed friendly. Her skinny, claw-like hand reached out and caught Eliza by the forearm.

'D'you hear me?' she said in a low threatening tone. 'You'd be best away from that house.'

'Dear me, why?' Eliza was intrigued. 'Why? What is wrong with that house?'

'I'm not saying.' The woman refused to be drawn. She turned away. 'Will your friend be wanting ribbons?'

'I just wondered about the house,' Eliza persisted. 'It must at one time have been a beautiful house—there are such elegant ceilings, like those I've seen in a grand house in Edinburgh.'

'Mind what I say.' Mistress Mackay's voice now seemed menacing. 'You'd be best away from that house.'

Eliza sighed. There was to be no more information from this strange old woman. She turned to where Catriona was still looking over the ribbons.

'I think,' Catriona said slowly, 'I take this. To trim a bonnet.' She held up a length of dark-blue silk ribbon.

'That will look very fine,' Eliza said.

'I have some money.' Catriona fumbled in her reticule.

It was then that the door was flung open.

'Good day to you, Morag.' The man who stood in the doorway swept off his hat. 'I've come about . . .' his voice drained away, and he stood staring at the two girls. 'Well, two fine young ladies.'

Eliza did not stop to hear the sneer in his tone. 'Come!' She grabbed Catriona by the arm. 'Leave these ribbons. Come, quick!'

As they pulled the door to, she could hear the man's voice, 'There are messages, Morag, are there not?'

SOMEWHERE SAFE

Catriona was bewildered.

'But what . . .?' she stammered.

'Come away, quickly!' Eliza half dragged her out of the shop, stumbling over the step.

'Run!' she told Catriona as soon as they were outside. 'As fast as you can!'

She grabbed Catriona's hand and they ran

68

along the narrow street. Eliza had no idea where they could go. Was it safe to go back to Shore House?

'Please!' Catriona protested. Eliza stopped for breath. She was all too aware that Catriona could not run far—her boots were fashionable, but not at all practical, and Eliza realised that her friend was probably not fit enough for such exercise. Already Catriona leaned against a wall, her hand to her heart and breathing rapidly.

'Oh, what am I to do!' Eliza looked round desperately.

'What is it? What is wrong?' Catriona clasped her hands.

'That man in the draper's,' Eliza said grimly. 'I have seen him before.'

Now, she felt, was not the time to explain how and where she had seen the mysterious stranger.

'He is dangerous. Trust me.'

She half pushed Catriona round a corner, until they were in the shelter of a narrow vennel. Anxiously, Eliza peered round the corner. There was no sign of the stranger. But she knew now that he must have followed them along the street. It was no accident that he had appeared in the draper's shop. And that strange old woman was somehow bound up in the whole affair.

'Whit are ye daein' here?'

Eliza whirled round.

'Oh, you gave me such a start!'

Robbie had appeared from the entrance to the vennel. Untidy and shabby as he was, he seemed to Eliza like a messenger of the gods.

'I am so thankful to see you.' She gasped. 'You can't think how glad.'

She took a deep breath.

'I cannot explain now, but it's not safe for us to return to Shore House, not just yet. Is there anywhere we would be safe, just for a little while?'

'Oh, aye.' Robbie was not a bit put out. 'I bide wi' ma sister. Her hoose is nearby.'

'Then can we wait there?'

It was clear that Catriona did not understand what was taking place, but she recognised that Robbie was their friend.

'Come away.' Robbie led the way along the vennel. 'It's just the back o' here.'

His sister's home was a small house in a row of houses, but it was clean, with a front step that had clearly been scrubbed that morning. Inside, a fire smouldered in the grate, sending out billowing smoke across the room. There was a plain deal table, a couple of upright chairs and only one armchair by the fire. In it sat an old man, puffing at a pipe. As Robbie led the two girls inside, a young woman turned from the sink.

'Save us, Robbie!' she said. 'Wha have ye brocht hame noo?'

'I apologise,' Eliza said, stepping forward.

70

'We are intruding. But we are in some trouble, and need to wait somewhere safe for a little while. Your brother has offered to bring us here. My name is Eliza Dunlop and this is Miss Catriona Stuart.'

'I'm Katherine,' the young woman said, 'but they ca' me Kate.' She apologised. 'The fire's smoking. But I'll open the door and it'll soon clear.' She went on. 'He's an awful laddie, that brither o' mine.' She smiled fondly at Robbie. 'Now come awa' in. It's maybe no what you're used tae, but ye're welcome tae wait here a whilie.'

She turned to the old man in the chair.

'Uncle, can ye no gie the ladies a seat?'

'Oh, please, no!' Eliza said. 'We're giving you trouble.'

'He bides wi' us,' Robbie's sister explained 'But he canna walk far.'

The old man waved his stick and pointed to his wooden leg.

'I was injured at Waterloo,' he said, with a note of fierce pride in his voice.

'You must have been very brave,' Eliza said gently.

'Here,' Robbie's sister said. 'Sit ye down.' She drew the two upright chairs forward.

'You are very kind.'

'Ye'll tak something?' Kate asked. 'We've no' that much tae offer, but there's scones, new baked . . . '

'Thank you.' Eliza felt it would be churlish

71

to refuse. And Kate's scones—fresh from the girdle—were very good.

Robbie, who had been rather quiet, ate two of the scones right away and said, with his mouth full, 'They're from Shore Hoose.'

'Oh?' Kate's eyebrows rose. 'Is that so?'

There was a silence, interrupted by a loud cry.

'Och, it's just the bairn,' Kate told them calmly.

She turned to the wooden cradle, which Eliza had not noticed.

'Noo, whit ails ye?' She rocked the cradle with her foot, and crooned at the infant.

But the baby only howled louder and, with a sigh, Kate gathered the child up with one hand, and held him in the crook of her arm, while she stirred the soup on the fire with the other hand.

'I hold baby?' Catriona asked timidly.

'Thank ye kindly, miss. He's a fine wee laddie. He doesna usually greet.'

Catriona cradled the baby in her arms, and seemed perfectly at home in the poor surroundings.

Eliza, watching Catriona, was surprised to see how gently she held the child, and how tenderly she rocked him

'My man's awa at the fishing,' Kate explained. 'And his wee lad will be a gey bit bigger by the time he gets back home.'

Eliza, looking round the dark, stuffy room

with the box bed in the corner, thought how different it was from the grand house in Edinburgh, or even Shore House. She had never been in a home like this. It smelled of damp, and there was little furniture.

There was only one small window, which looked out on to the vennel. But Kate did not seem the least bit disturbed at having to entertain two unexpected visitors—visitors who, Robbie had told her, were in desperate need of shelter.

'That's a fine cradle,' Eliza said, trying to think of something to say. The baby had stopped crying now and was gazing up at Catriona with solemn blue eyes.

'Uncle Will made it—did ye no'?' Kate addressed the man in the chair. 'He canna do much but hirple along the road tae meet his cronies. Is that no' richt? He maks fine spurtles—they're spoons tae stir the porridge, wi' braw carvings.'

Eliza knelt down by the old man. She saw with a shock that he was not really old, but badly crippled.

'You are a craftsman,' she said.

'Aye. I'm no bad wi' my hands, but I'd sooner be at the fishing with her man.'

'You fought at Waterloo,' Eliza said.

'Aye, that was a bad business for all that we won.' He lapsed into silence, and Eliza wondered about Kate.

She watched her, a tall, sturdy woman with

73

rosy cheeks and bright eyes. Maybe a year or so older than she was, she thought, but she looked much older. What a hard life it must be; her husband away at sea, caring for a baby and a young brother, not to mention an uncle who was unable to work. How did she manage? For a moment Eliza forgot her own anxieties.

Meantime, Robbie continued to dart back and forward to the door, looking out into the street.

'It was a tall man, black hair, black brows,' Eliza began.

'I've seen him,' Robbie said briefly. 'Maister Jamie said I was to look out for him.'

Eliza explained how he had come into the draper's and how she and Catriona had escaped from the shop.

'I'll away round, miss.' Robbie said importantly. 'I'll tak' a look. He's maybe gone by now.'

Soon afterwards, he reappeared. By now Eliza was in conversation with Uncle about his carving. Catriona had rocked the baby to sleep and gently put him back in his cradle.

'Ye're safe now,' Robbie assured them. 'He's no' there. But I'll gang wi' ye back to Shore Hoose. He'll no bother ye there once ye're indoors.'

'Thank you.' Eliza turned to Kate. 'You have helped us such a great deal. We were really alarmed.'

'It's naething.' Kate smiled. 'Ye're welcome tae come here whenever you like.'

Catriona smiled and kissed the baby

'Such a fine child.'

During the hour or so they had been in the house, Eliza noticed that Catriona seemed quite oblivious to the poor and shabby conditions of the room. Oh, it was clean and Kate herself was scrubbed and wholesome. And Eliza noticed the holes in the knees of Robbie's trousers had been patched. Kate was clearly doing her best to keep her little family together. But Catriona might have been in the grandest drawing-room in Edinburgh. She nodded and smiled at Kate and the old uncle, laying her hand gently on his arm.

Suddenly Eliza felt a little ashamed.

She was fortunate. She had a roof over her head, clothes to wear, and enough food to eat, and they had so little.

And Catriona, sitting there in her velvet cloak and fine soft leather boots seemed perfectly at home.

It had, Eliza thought, been a very strange morning.

A PLEASANT EVENING

When Eliza told Maggie of their adventure, Maggie looked serious.

'I hope you will take care,' she said. 'You know we are here to help if there is any danger.'

'I know.' Eliza smiled at her new friend. 'But we had an interesting visit when Robbie took us to his home.'

'Kate does wondrous well,' Maggie said. 'And Robbie is a fine lad and helps her a good deal. But I am afraid he is no scholar. He no longer goes to school and my father has tried to teach him, but he has no interest in his books. Now my father is trying to find him a place as an apprentice. But Robbie is quite determined to go to sea, like his father, and you can imagine that Kate is fearful for him. It is a hard and dangerous calling.'

Eliza thought how kindly the minister was, although at first sight you might have thought he was absent-minded, deep in his books and commentaries.

'We would like you to come to dinner,' Maggie went on, 'before Jamie goes back to Edinburgh next week.'

'He is going back to Edinburgh so soon?' Eliza burst out before she could help herself

'Yes, he is now fully recovered,' Maggie said cheerfully. 'And before he goes we would like to invite you and Miss Catriona to dine with us. I am making a rabbit and pork pie. It is a specialty of Fife, and Miss Catriona might enjoy it. And,' she added frankly, 'it is one of the few dishes I can make successfully. My

76

father—God bless him—rarely notices what he eats, and our maid, Isla, can cook only the plainest of fare.'

'I am quite accustomed to plain fare,' Eliza said, 'and we will be very pleased to accept your invitation. Only,' she hesitated, 'I may find it hard to explain to Mistress Kilbain. Not that I have to seek her permission, but she is keeping a close guard on Catriona.'

'My father will write a letter of invitation,' Maggie decided, 'and then she cannot possibly refuse to let you come to us.'

The next day Maggie arrived at the door of Shore House with a letter addressed to Mistress Kilbain.

'It is from my father,' she said when the housekeeper opened the door.

The woman took the envelope and looked at it suspiciously.

'So, what is this?' She turned the envelope over and sniffed.

'It is addressed to you,' Maggie said.

'And what use is that,' the housekeeper asked sharply, 'seeing as I canna read or write.'

'Oh, really?' Maggie tried to hide her surprise. How did the woman manage to decipher the butcher's bill, or a receipt, for example? Then, she thought, the housekeeper was so sharp, few tradesmen would get the better of her, whether she could read or not.

'Then I will read it to you.' Before the woman had time to protest, Maggie had ripped open the envelope.

'It says,' she began, *'Dear Mistress Kilbain, It would give me great pleasure if you would allow Miss Eliza Dunlop and Miss Catriona Stuart to dine with me and my family on Thursday. We dine at 6 p.m.*

'I will ensure that the two young ladies are safely conveyed to the manse and brought back to Shore House.

'Trusting that this is agreeable to you, I am yours respectfully, Joshua Grieve.'

'Yours respectfully.' Something that might have been taken for a smile passed over Mistress Kilbain's face.

'Yours respectfully—fancy him writing that to me, and him a minister of the cloth.'

'So you are agreeable, then?' Maggie asked hopefully. She rushed on without waiting for a reply. 'My brother will call for them and escort them to the manse.'

*   *   *

'It was our father's letter that persuaded her,' Maggie said that Thursday evening to Eliza, as she welcomed them to the manse. The two girls took off their cloaks and handed them to the little maid. 'She was quite impressed.'

Jamie was all smiles and welcome.

'I hope you are feeling much better,' Eliza said rather shyly.

'Indeed I am,' he returned, with a little bow

78

in her direction. 'And it is time I returned to Edinburgh. Though I should dearly like to stay here, especially now that two such charming visitors have arrived in the village.'

Eliza blushed. Catriona, whose English was not yet up to coping with such compliments, was silent. She had been rather quiet the past few days, Eliza had noticed. Perhaps she was downhearted at the thought of Jamie's departure.

'But there,' Jamie said cheerfully, 'we mustn't think of partings, but simply enjoy the evening together. I promise that you will enjoy the rabbit and pork pie that Maggie has made.'

When they had gathered round the table, and the minister had said grace, Maggie carried in the pie with an air of triumph.

'There!' she said. 'I hope it tastes good.'

Jamie sniffed appreciatively.

'Would that the food in my Edinburgh lodgings were half as good as this,' he said.

'Come now.' Maggie laughed as she dished up the pie.

Eliza thought how pleasant it must be to have a brother like Jamie, and how well brother and sister agreed together.

Everyone voted it was quite the best pie that Maggie had made.

'There is some left,' Maggie said. 'Would anyone like another helping?'

They all said they had eaten well enough.

'Then there will be some left over for

Robbie when he calls tomorrow.' Maggie smiled.

'Oh!' Eliza exclaimed. 'We have met Robbie's sister and the uncle and the baby.' She told the gathering about the adventure a few days previously.

Jamie listened, agog. His father looked serious.

'I wish something could be done for that family,' he said. 'The lad, Robbie, is bright and would learn a trade quickly. But he is intent on going to the fishing, and I'm afraid it is a hard and dangerous calling. Though,' he added, as if to himself, 'who am I to try to stop him, when the disciples themselves were fishermen.'

Eliza broke into the silence.

'That was not the only person we met. In the draper's shop there was a very old, bent woman, who spoke as if she had only just come from the Isles.'

Jamie smiled.

'Ah, yes,' he said. 'Morag Mackay. So you've met Morag! She is a character indeed.'

'How did she come here?'

'Her family followed the Prince,' Jamie informed her. 'Though she was but a babe at the time of the Rising, she has grown up with the Jacobites. For two pins, old as she is, I do believe she would follow the flag once more. She came south to marry a fisherman and was widowed many years ago. But I'm certain she still believes the Stuarts will come into their own.'

'And the stranger?' Eliza asked. 'I have seen him before. Why would he follow us, and why did he seem to know old Morag?' She explained what had happened and what she had overheard. 'That man mentioned that Morag had messages for him.'

Jamie looked thoughtful.

'It is all to do with the Jacobite cause, I am certain,' Jamie told her. 'When the Prince left these shores for good, it was, as they said "the end of an auld sang".'

'Come now,' their father said. 'That is history. We will not speak of past battles. Both sides have been reconciled a long time ago. There is no enmity now between Stuart and Hanover. Indeed, our present King and his father have behaved generously towards Charles and his brother.' He reached out for a handful of nuts from the silver dish on the table.

'As we have these two young ladies as guests, why do we not have some music?' he suggested.

'An excellent idea! Do you sing, Miss Catriona?' Jamie asked.

Catriona shook her head.

'A very little.'

'Oh, you do sing, and very well, too,' Eliza spoke up. 'The other day you sang some little folk song to the baby while Kate was working. And I heard you singing an old song very

81

sweetly just the other day.'

The evening's entertainment was very pleasant, Eliza thought afterwards. Maggie sang, in a clear tuneful soprano, one or two ballads. Her brother sang some of Burns's most beautiful songs. Eliza thought when he sang 'Ae Fond Kiss' that he looked at Catriona. But perhaps she was wrong and was simply imagining things.

Catriona was persuaded to sing two little French folk songs, to loud applause from the company. She sat down, blushing shyly.

'Oh, well done, Miss Catriona!' Jamie said, applauding.

'Now, Miss Eliza, it's your turn.'

'Alas, I cannot sing. Not a note. The corncrake himself,' Eliza stated dramatically, 'has a purer singing voice than I.'

'You will not? I had hoped we might sing duets together.'

Eliza shook her head, laughing.

'You would not invite me again if you heard my voice,' she said.

'In that case,' Jamie said. 'I must accept your decision, as we should not want to be deprived of your company at some future date.' He smiled at her.

Eliza blushed. She wished that she had met more young men, and then she would know how to flirt.

She was sorry when the evening drew to an end, and Jamie escorted her and Catriona back to Shore House.

'See what a fine summer night it is,' he said, as they paused by the sea wall, looking out over the waves. 'Let us hope it's as fine for the King when he arrives at Leith.'

'When will that be?' Eliza had almost forgotten about the King's visit to Edinburgh.

'It depends on the weather. He sails from Greenwich on Saturday,' Jamie replied. 'Already the city is agog. Sir Walter Scott has planned all sorts of events; there are plans for bonfires and parades and other festivities. As for the ladies, they have been planning for months what they will wear. Trade has been brisk for some time for the dressmakers and shoemakers.'

'I should dearly like to see the spectacle,' Eliza commented, forgetting that she had set sail for Fife with the desire never to set foot in Edinburgh again.

'Perhaps you will.' Jamie broke off. 'See, out there!'

'I can see nothing.' Eliza drew her shawl around her.

'The dark shapes. They are small boats on the way out to load from a larger ship. They're bringing back casks of rum and gin.'

'Smugglers!' Eliza cried in astonishment. 'You said they landed contraband, but I didn't expect to see them so close.'

'Oh, yes, and I think you'll find that some casks find their way into Shore House, through that side passage.'

'Well!' Eliza was astonished.

Catriona shivered, and Jamie turned to her.

'Come, you are feeling the chill of the night air.' He paused at the door. 'If I do not see you before I go, I will not be away for long. And you may be sure I will send messages from Edinburgh.'

He bowed to them both, and was gone. After Catriona had gone indoors, Eliza stood for a moment or two, looking after him. Then, with a sigh, she, too, turned and went inside.

FEVER

The days after Jamie's departure for Edinburgh seemed empty. Now that there was no chance of meeting the stocky, sandy-haired figure in the street, or hearing his cheerful laugh as he teased his sister, Eliza was surprised how quickly he had become part of their lives.

She wondered if Catriona was missing Jamie, too. But of course she was. Hadn't Eliza seen the way she lowered her eyes, blushing when he spoke to her. Hadn't she seen the way Jamie offered her his arm as they walked back to Shore House? Hadn't she heard the gentle tones in which he bade her to take special care?

Eliza found herself thinking a good deal about Jamie.

Stop it, she thought firmly to herself. She had obviously read too many novels. In any case, she thought, what did she have to offer any suitor? She was no beauty, and she had no money. Maybe some day, someone would come along who needed a wife, who would see past such things.

She tried hard to think of her good points, but she could not, in all honesty, think of very many. She was optimistic by nature, she was physically strong and could work hard. She was reasonably well read, though she had not had much formal education, and she read everything that she could find.

She was a cheerful, hard-working girl who liked reading. It was not much to offer, compared with the beautiful, accomplished young ladies that Jamie would meet in Edinburgh, who could play the piano and sing, and were always dressed in the height of fashion. She thought, a little sadly, that she would never be beautiful or accomplished. So forget about Jamie, she told herself briskly. He would never look at her anyway.

Still, every few days she waited for a message from him. At last she plucked up her courage and asked Maggie.

'Is there any word from your brother?' She tried to make her tone as casual as possible.

Maggie shook her head.

'No, but you may be sure he is not idle. I have never known Jamie to be idle in all his life. He is always finding out, asking questions. I am certain we will hear from him soon. He is like a terrier when he is finding out things,' she said proudly.

So there was nothing to be done, Eliza thought, nothing except wait patiently to hear from Jamie. And she knew she had to be constantly on watch, looking over her shoulder for the stranger in black.

'It is much too good to be indoors,' she told Catriona one fine August morning. How she longed to be away from this gaunt, damp house with its oppressive atmosphere, out enjoying the warmth of the summer sunshine, the light sparkling on the waves, and breathing in the fresh, salty air.

As usual, the two girls strolled along the narrow lane to the harbour, pausing only to look in the window of the baker's shop. Suddenly there was a voice behind them.

'Miss! Miss!'

Eliza, alarmed, whirled round.

'Oh, Robbie, you did give me a start!'

Robbie, she saw, was not his usual self. Gone was the broad grin, the cheeky expression.

'Is something the matter?' she asked, concerned.

'It's ma sister. She's no weel. I'm away tae get milk for the bairn.'

'We'll come right away.' Eliza grasped Catriona by the arm, and they hurried along the street and turned sharply into the narrow vennel. Eliza drew a deep breath. No wonder poor Kate was ill, living in such a dark, damp place.

She hesitated for a moment. Perhaps she shouldn't take Catriona into a house of sickness.

'You wait here,' she tried to explain. 'Perhaps she is infectious.'

Catriona shook her head.

'I come with you,' she said firmly.

Inside the room was hot and stuffy, the windows tightly closed. The uncle was sitting in his chair by the fire and the baby's cries rose shrilly. In the box bed lay Kate, very quietly, not tossing and turning. Eliza felt a moment of panic as she approached the bed and saw how flushed and feverish the woman was.

She felt herself gently nudged aside as Catriona put a hand on Kate's brow.

'She has a high fever,' she said. 'How long has she been like this?'

She turned to the uncle.

'She's been no weel a couple of days,' he said.

'And have you had the doctor?' Eliza asked

'Doctors!' He spat into the fire. 'Doctors cost money!'

Meantime Catriona had found a basin at the sink and filled it with water. She dipped into the water a clean lawn handkerchief, and gently sponged the woman's brow, talking to her all the while.

'Is there food in the house?' Eliza asked the uncle.

'No' much,' he said morosely. 'She canna eat.'

'In that case,' Eliza drew out her purse, 'I will send Robbie for some provisions. Soup, I think.' She turned to the sink where dishes had been piled high. With a little grimace, she took off her cloak and rolled up her sleeves. She filled a pot with water and set it on the fire.

Meantime, on the bed, the woman tossed and groaned a little.

'Is she very ill?' Eliza asked Catriona in a whisper.

'She has a fever,' Catriona replied. 'When the fever goes, then she will recover.' She continued sponging Kate's face.

There was a clatter at the door and Robbie peered round.

'Is she still no weel?'

Eliza turned.

'She is far from well, and we will need your help to run messages.' She took the can of milk, then picked up the baby from its cradle. Red-faced, bawling with rage and hunger, the child squirmed in her arms.

'Feugh!' Eliza realised that the child needed to be changed. 'I will feed you first,' she decided.

'There's a wee cup wi a spout,' Robbie told her.

'That will do well.' Eliza poured a little milk into the cup and gently persuaded the baby to feed.

She looked round the room. The uncle was not able to be of much help, she decided. And clearly Kate was likely to be ill for some time, if she recovered.

But, she decided quickly, now was not the time to think of such things.

'Robbie,' she told him, 'you must run to the butcher's. See if he has a bone to spare, and then to the baker's for a loaf We will need potatoes and leeks for the broth.

'And then you must run to the manse. Tell Miss Maggie that your sister is ill. She will know what to do.' Suddenly, looking round the poor shabby room, she felt a sense of relief. Maggie would help.

As soon as Robbie knocked at the door and gasped out his message, Maggie became brisk and business-like.

'Wait there,' she told the boy. 'I will need you to carry some things.'

'Now,' she said to herself, 'we shall need . . .' Her mind raced over all that might be required, and she began whirling round the manse, gathering blankets, a clean sheet, fresh pillowslips, fresh eggs from the hens that clucked around the back door, and a piece of cheese.

'My dear, what is the matter?' The minister came out of his study, his white hair ruffled, as if he had been some distance away from everyday events. As indeed he had been, steeped in his work, a commentary on the book of Deuteronomy.

'Father, just for today you will have to make do with bannocks and cheese.' Maggie explained what had happened. She added, 'And I will take some vegetables from the garden, if I may.'

'But of course, my dear Maggie, you must go to that poor family at once.' He looked troubled. 'Shall I come with you?'

'No, no,' Maggie said hastily. 'Perhaps later you could visit.'

'Indeed.' He smiled benignly. 'You are most certainly a good soul, daughter. A very present help in time of trouble.'

Maggie knew that her father was remote from the everyday cares of the world. Much of the time he was back in the world of the Old Testament. But she knew, too, that he was welcomed in every house in the village, and where there was trouble, people opened their doors to him and felt comforted by his gentle voice.

But now she gave hasty instructions to the little maid, who was standing wide-eyed.

'Isla,' she told her, 'do make sure that my father eats the bannocks and cheese at noon.' As she spoke she was pouring into a bowl the

90

harvest broth, made of good fresh vegetables from the manse garden. She knew very well that it did not matter to the minister what he ate.

'There,' she said, as she handed the bedding to Robbie, 'I hope these will be of some use. Now don't let's waste any more time.' She set off briskly, followed by Robbie, who was almost running to catch up with her.

'Oh, Maggie!' Eliza turned from the sink when her friend arrived. 'I am so glad to see you.'

Maggie unpacked the basket.

'This is good broth,' she said. 'Perhaps Kate could take a little.' She glanced round.

Catriona was bent over the sick woman, talking to her in a gentle voice. From time to time Kate struggled to speak, and Catriona leaned closer, to hear what she was trying to say.

'The bairn . . .' Kate whispered.

'Don't be afraid,' Catriona said, stroking the woman's thin hand that lay on the coverlet. 'There is milk and Maggie has brought soup.'

Kate sank back with the ghost of a smile as Catriona continued to sponge her forehead.

At the sink, Eliza was scouring pots, setting a pan of hot water on the fire. Maggie looked round approvingly.

'How long has she been like this?' she asked Robbie in a low voice.

'A day, mebbe more.'

'If she is no better by tomorrow, we will send for the doctor,' she decided.

'We've nae money for doctors,' Robbie objected.

'Never heed that.' She turned to the man sitting by the fire, who had so far said nothing.

'I'm nae muckle use, miss,' he said suddenly. 'I canna walk ony distance, or gang for messages, or dae onything aboot the house.'

Eliza moved forward from the sink.

'You can see to the fire,' she said. She shivered. How damp the house was. No wonder Kate was ill. 'And Robbie can bring in firewood. There is plenty of wood on the shore.'

'Aye,' Robbie said, his face brightening. 'I'll get away down there.'

'And,' Eliza went on talking to the uncle, 'you can carve those fine spurtles and toys for children. Animals from Noah's Ark. And you could sell them.'

'I could that. We could dae wi' the money.'

It seemed a very long day. Eliza brought a bowl of tepid water and watched as Catriona washed the sick woman's face and hands, and smoothed the fresh pillow slip.

She gazed anxiously as Kate tossed, muttering to herself in her fever. She dandled the baby on her lap and fed the child sips of broth.

'We will come back tomorrow,' Eliza told Robbie. 'Meantime, you must run to the manse immediately if your sister seems worse.'

'Aye,' he muttered.

She put a reassuring hand on his shoulder.

'You have been a great help,' she told him. 'Now, you must sponge her brow as Miss Catriona has done, and when she is stronger she may take a few sips of broth.'

Maggie had laid out soup and bannocks for Robbie and his uncle, and the baby, fed and clean, lay contentedly in the cradle.

On the way back to Shore House, Eliza glanced sideways at Catriona.

'Will Kate recover, do you think?'

'I hope so.' Catriona looked serious. 'She is strong.'

'You know.' Eliza hesitated, not wanting to seem curious, 'You know how to care for sick people.'

'In the convent,' Catriona explained, 'I often helped in the infirmary. I cared for Sister Ignatia, until she . . .'

Eliza was silent, but she asked herself, how could I have been so mistaken? She had thought Catriona was simply a young lady, gently raised in the convent. And how she had envied the other girl's beautiful clothes.

And yet, seeing how calmly and with what a kindly touch Catriona had cared for Kate, she knew there was more to her friend. She was someone who had worked as a nurse, who had cared for a dying woman. She looked sideways again at Catriona's calm expression.

'I wonder,' Eliza said, 'if Mistress Kilbain has noticed our absence.' She grimaced. 'I expect she is on the doorstep in a rage. And complaining that dinner will be spoiled.'

But there was no sign of the housekeeper, and the house was very still. The two girls looked at each other, questioning.

'Where is she?' Catriona wondered. There was no sign of activity, and they stole along the passage towards the kitchen. 'Look!' Catriona said in a whisper.

They stood at the open door, gazing in astonishment.

The housekeeper was slumped on a chair by the table, her head resting on her arms. She was snoring. Eliza tiptoed forward and put a hand on the woman's arm, but there was no response.

'She is asleep,' Catriona said in a low tone.

'Deeply asleep,' Eliza replied with a smile, as she lifted the empty gin bottle from the table.

'See! She is drunk.'

'The smugglers,' she added. 'They bring the gin and brandy in by the side door. And Madam has a drink or two, or more.' She gave a half smile. 'Come,' she said, 'let's leave her to sleep it off. She will have a sore head in the morning. And you and I must dine on fruit and cheese.'

'Very well.' Catriona smiled and the two girls tiptoed out of the kitchen.

SANDY'S RETURN

'We shall be going out today,' Eliza told Mistress Kilbain next morning. 'So we may need dinner a little later.'

She half smiled to herself, thinking how afraid she had been of the housekeeper when she first came to Shore House a few weeks ago. It was astonishing, she thought, how much had happened in that time. As she dressed, she wondered how Kate was doing. She and Catriona would go along immediately they had finished breakfast.

'She's a wee bit better,' Robbie said as he answered the door. 'I sat up in the night wi' her.'

'Well done.' Eliza patted him on the shoulder. Catriona laid a hand on the sick woman's forehead.

'She has a fever still,' she said in a low voice. 'But I think she is not as hot as before.'

Eliza busied herself with tidying the room and washing the dishes. She swept the floor and opened the window to let in the fresh air. Before long, Maggie arrived, carrying a basket covered with a white napkin.

'I have brought some of my calves' foot jelly,' she said. 'Perhaps Kate could take a little.'

Kate tried to thank her.

'Lie still,' Maggie said briskly to Kate. 'And get well.'

There was a good deal to do, what with tending to Kate and the baby, and making sure that Uncle was comfortable. 'I'm nae use tae ye,' he said fretfully. 'I canna dae naething tae help.'

Eliza put a hand on his arm.

'Don't you be thinking that,' she said kindly. 'You will be a grand support to Kate when she's well.'

Later that day, Maggie spoke in a low whisper to Eliza.

'How does she do?'

'A little better,' Eliza replied. 'Once the fever has gone she will be weak, and will have to regain strength.'

Maggie nodded.

'I am surprised,' she said, 'that Catriona is such a good nurse.'

'She has nursed before,' Eliza informed her. 'I understand she cared for one of the sisters in the convent.'

'Ah.' Maggie was silent for a moment. 'We know very little about her, apart from her history which my father has discovered. But what we do know, I like. She is quiet and modest, and has a sweet nature, I think. Our family are glad to have met her.'

And, Eliza thought, though she did not say so out loud, Jamie likes her very much. In fact, I think he must be falling in love with her. You do hear of such things—people falling in love at first sight. I wonder how she feels about Jamie. It would be very suitable, this match.

She gave a little sigh and very determinedly put aside all her thoughts of Jamie. He was nothing to her, he was Maggie's brother, and someone who would be a support to Catriona in this strange situation.

The past few days had almost driven from her mind the awareness of danger. Now she asked Maggie, 'I suppose there is no word from your brother?'

Maggie shook her head.

'Nothing. But don't be concerned. I know him. He will not be wasting time. He will send a message as soon as he can.' She laid a hand on Eliza's arm. 'And as soon as I hear from him, I will let you know.'

Eliza was somewhat reassured by this. She decided she must keep Catriona safe—not just because Jamie had warned her of danger, but because he had a special reason for caring for Catriona's safety.

During the next week Kate gradually recovered. The fever gone, she was able to get out of bed and sit, still looking white and drawn, by the fireside. One day, when Eliza and Catriona visited, she called out to them.

'See, I'm out of my bed.'

'You're getting better.' Eliza smiled at her.

'You've been right kind,' Kate said. 'Miss Stuart, too. And Miss Maggie from the manse.'

'Now you must get well and strong,' Eliza said.

'It's no' like me tae be ill,' Kate said. 'But wi' that guid broth and the calves' foot jelly, I'll soon be on my feet.'

But before she was quite herself again, the little house was thrown into turmoil. One evening, the door burst open, and the room was all of a sudden full of life, and a breeze of salty air seemed to follow the huge figure who took up the doorway.

'I'm back, lass!' he roared. 'Back hame!'

'Sandy! It's you!' Kate's face brightened.

Eliza hung back, staring at the bearded figure who seemed to carry with him all the sounds and smells of the North Sea into that cramped little room.

'So what's this?' He realised that Kate was sitting in a chair by the fire, and that she looked thin and pale. 'Are ye ill, lass?' He put a hand on her shoulder.

Kate explained.

'But I'm some better now,' she said, smiling at him

'Thanks to good friends.'

'And I didna ken,' he said remorsefully. 'Or I'd never have left you.'

'Och, awa wi' ye.' She smiled up at him weakly.

When Sandy learned that Eliza and Catriona had helped to care for Kate, he wrung them both by the hand.

'I'm no sure how I can thank ye two 'eddies,' he said, a catch in his voice.

'We were glad to help.' Eliza assured him. 'Maggie, too. Miss Grieve, that is, the minister's daughter. She has brought food and fresh sheets, and her own calves' foot jelly, and other food.'

'I ken her fine,' he said. 'And I thank you all,' he added with dignity. Then, 'How's Robbie?'

'He's been a grand help,' Eliza assured him. 'Though I know he would have liked to be at sea, instead of running errands for women.'

The big man smiled.

'He'll mak a fisherman one day. And as to that . . .' he pulled out a canvas bag '. . . there's a couple o' herring. We'd good catches.'

'Herring in oatmeal.' Uncle spoke from his seat by the fire. 'The best dish ever.'

'You must be hungry.' Eliza set the pan on the fire, while Catriona put out on the table the bannocks and butter, and a jug of ale.

As he ate, Sandy told them between mouthfuls of the past weeks at sea, where the herring were running, how they'd run into a storm off Arbroath.

'My, but it's fine to be hame,' he said, leaning back in his chair. 'And the *Sarah Ann's* safe in harbour. Mind you, there's a wheen o' the herring drifters back in Kingsferry. Fowk aye say that ye can walk from ane tae the ither without getting yer feet wet!' He laughed.

99

Then he paused. 'I ken near ilka boat in the fleet. Still, when we cam into port, there was ane I'd not seen afore. A wee fishing boat. No' near the size o' the drifters. The *Clementina*, they ca'd her. Ye get so ye notice a strange craft in the harbour.'

He wiped his plate with a piece of bread. 'That was grand, miss.'

A strange fishing boat, Eliza thought, in the harbour. She felt a shiver of fear.

AUNT BESS

During the next week, while they waited for news at the manse, Maggie continued to visit Kate and family.

'Ye're a grand help,' Kate said admiringly. 'For all ye're a minister's daughter, and used to grander surroundings.'

'Oh, fiddle-de-dee!' Maggie scoffed. 'We are not grand at all. Besides,' she added, 'there is nothing I like better than working in a house. Cleaning, scrubbing floors, making soup, keeping all fresh and welcoming.'

'Ye should hae a hame o' yer ain,' Kate said.

'Oh,' Maggie replied, 'that is not likely. But I am quite content looking after my father and Jamie, my brother, when he is at home. Not that my father would notice what he ate,' she added. 'He is too bound up in his books and sermons.'

'I liked it fine when he cam here,' Kate said shyly. 'I felt the better o' his visit.'

'I'll tell him that.' Maggie smiled at her.

Kate had looked more cheerful since Sandy's arrival home. Not that he was a peaceful presence in the house—he roared in with his hearty laugh, picked up the baby and danced around the room with him. But with Kate he was tender and watchful. It must be fine, Maggie thought wistfully, to have someone who cared as much for you. Though there was nothing sentimental about Sandy. No embraces, no fine words, just continuous concern and caring.

One day he brought a friend to visit, a giant of a man, broad as he was tall, with a huge red beard. Maggie was sitting by the fireside, cradling the baby and singing to him an old Scots song. She looked up, surprised.

'You'll not mind if I bring a friend in for a bite,' Sandy addressed his wife. 'He's the captain of a vessel moored in the harbour.'

Kate rose from her seat.

'You are welcome, sir,' she said.

'I thank ye, mistress,' the man said in a deep bass voice. 'I hope I do not intrude.'

Maggie, sitting by the fireside, was slightly puzzled by his accent. Surely he was not from Fife?

'Erik's from Norway,' Sandy said, slapping his friend on the back. 'They're taking on crew

101

here before they sail to Orkney.'

'You are welcome,' Kate said in her slow dignified way. 'I hope you will take a bite with us.'

'And this is your uncle?' the tall man said. 'Who was at Waterloo, so I hear.'

The old man's eyes lit up with pleasure at being recognised.

'I would like to hear your account of the battle,' Erik said, shaking Uncle by the hand.

'And this lady? Your sister?' he asked Kate.

'No, but she has been like a sister to me,' Kate told him. 'She is the daughter of our minister, and she and her friends saved my life when I was ill with fever.'

'Indeed,' the tall man said gravely and bowed to Maggie. 'A true friend.'

*   *   *

What had happened to Jamie? For some days now, Eliza had expected a message. Certainly Maggie had said that he would be working quietly, investigating this strange business, and they were sure to hear from him before long. Eliza knew in her heart that she could trust Jamie—hadn't she observed often how calm and steadfast he was? But all the same, she wished that he would get in touch.

Jamie, meantime, had not been idle. As soon as he arrived in Edinburgh, he talked to friends who knew Mr Humbie.

'Be wary of him,' his friend Robert said, who shared a desk with Jamie. 'There is nothing definite of which he might be accused, but there are rumours of his business dealings, for example.'

'And have you heard,' Jamie asked him, 'whether he might be sympathetic to the Jacobite cause?'

Robert looked thoughtful.

'I would not be surprised,' he said. 'But surely there can be no harm in that. It is a very long time since there were Jacobite supporters in the city. Still I would be cautious about meeting him.'

'It is important that I meet him,' Jamie said. 'Even socially. I cannot tell you why but . . .'

He broke off.

His friend laughed.

'Ah, I see. There must be a young lady involved. This is intriguing.' He added, 'I won't ask any more. But, I beg you, be on your guard against Mr Humbie. He has a bad reputation in the city.'

Jamie decided there was only one thing to be done.

'Visit Aunt Bess,' he told himself. He made a face as he looked in the mirror, tying his stock with extra care.

He saw very little of Aunt Bess, who was his mother's sister, and lived in style in a grand house in Charlotte Square. Jamie was seldom invited and did not visit often. Uncle William was a quiet man, a businessman, who seldom said much beyond, 'Aye. That's right, Bess.' Jamie liked him and wished they had more opportunities to talk.

But Aunt Bess was quite different. Loud-spoken, dressed in the height of fashion, in expensive silks and flamboyant caps or headdresses of ostrich feathers, she was an imposing sight. She was, Jamie acknowledged, a snob, with ambitions to rise in society, but underneath he knew she had a generous heart.

Aunt Bess knew everyone. Her soirées were events attended by half of Edinburgh—the better half, she always said proudly. Jamie grimaced at the prospect. However, he was fairly sure that she would know Mr Humbie.

Now, he decided, he would call. He pulled at the brass bell outside the three-storey house and was admitted by a maidservant.

'Is your mistress in?'

'I'll find out.' The girl dropped a swift curtsey and disappeared.

A few minutes later she returned, and took Jamie's hat and gloves.

'She'll see you,' she announced, leading the way to the first floor drawing-room that overlooked the square. Jamie never failed to be impressed by the elegance of the room, the painted ceiling, the oil paintings, and the chairs upholstered in the finest brocade.

'Jamie! Well, this is a surprise!'

Aunt Bess rose from the sofa where she

had been half reclining. It was something of an effort, for she had become rather stout. Although it was still early in the day, she was dressed in a black and white striped taffeta, with a matching mob cap, trimmed with white lace.

'And what brings you here?' Aunt Bess was always direct.

'To see you, Aunt.' Jamie gave a little bow.

'Oh.' She bridled. 'You always did have a silver tongue in your head.'

'My father and sister ask to be remembered to you.'

'Indeed.' Aunt Bess's tone was a little frosty. 'And what is your father doing now? Still writing his sermons, I suppose.' She pursed her lips. 'I can never understand why your father is content to remain in such a backwater as Kingsferry.' She had been seriously displeased when her sister chose to marry the young minister, and even more so when they had settled in the small fishing town of Kingsferry. 'Poor Janet.'

Jamie was defensive.

'My mother was quite content.' He remembered the quiet, gentle woman who had told her children stories of witches and warlocks, and had sung them old ballads at bedtime. She had been nothing like Aunt Bess.

Aunt Bess sniffed, then turned to another grievance. 'And your sister? I don't suppose she moves much in society.'

'No, Maggie does not attend balls and levees, but she is always busy and active about the village.'

'A pity.' Aunt Bess sniffed. 'I would have her here, introduce her to people. She will need to make a good marriage, because I cannot think there is any money.'

Jamie shook his head.

'There is no money at all. But I think that does not matter to Maggie.'

'Does not matter?' Aunt Bess said sharply. 'Of course it matters. You are very unworldly, you and your sister. At least you have a profession,' she allowed.

'While you are here,' she added, 'I would like you to meet a few people. I am giving one of my soirées this week, for the King's visit. Such a shame that dear Rosa cannot take part in all the wonderful balls and levees this week. But there it is.'

'Rosa?' Jamie remembered a cousin, a lively, outspoken girl with a loud voice, but he had not seen her since her marriage.

'Yes, of course you remember her,' Aunt Bess said. 'She is staying here for the moment, until—' she paused delicately, 'she is brought to bed. Her husband is in the Guards and must attend on His Majesty.'

She went on.

'What a very exciting time, to be sure! What with the balls and receptions, and the bonfires to welcome the King. I should dearly love to be at Leith when the Royal George arrives. And how he must look forward to meeting the cream of Edinburgh society. I feel sorry,' she said with some satisfaction, 'for people who live in Glasgow. His Majesty will not be able to visit their city. And the Highlanders! Have you seen them?'

'I am but lately returned from Fife, madam,' Jamie put in.

'Ah, yes, I had forgotten. Fife . . .' she continued. 'They have come from all over the country in their tartans. How fine they look, marching about the city! It is all the doing of dear Sir Walter Scott. They tell me he sits daily in his study at Castle Street and people crowd in on him with requests which he deals with so patiently.'

'You know him, madam?' Jamie asked politely.

She hesitated.

'Not closely acquainted, but I do know him, and hope that he will be able to spare the time to come to my soirée on Sunday evening, the day the King arrives.'

Jamie knew that his aunt had not a great deal of interest in her late sister's family, and had more or less discarded any notion of trying to bring Maggie into society. But she still had ambitions for him, for her nephew, that he might somehow rise in Edinburgh circles. He smiled at her, recognising that under the veneer of snobbery, she was basically a good-hearted person.

'You know a great many people,' he said.

'I do,' she acknowledged with a little inclination of her head so that the feathers on her mob cap quivered.

'I wonder,' he said, trying to sound casual, 'if you have heard of a Mr Humbie. He is an Edinburgh advocate, with offices on North Bridge.'

'Indeed I have,' she said. 'A most distinguished lawyer. I have hopes that he will attend my soirée this Sunday.'

'Then I shall hope to meet him.'

'Seven o'clock promptly,' she told him. 'There are several young ladies I should like you to meet. The Misses Grant are coming from Rothiemurchus, and I feel sure their dear mother, who cannot be with them, would be glad if they could be introduced to some suitable young men.'

Jamie was about to respond politely, but Aunt Bess hurried on.

'I hope you will dress smartly,' she said firmly. 'I expect you to do me credit.'

'Yes, Aunt,' Jamie said meekly. He said goodbye, collected his hat and gloves and made his way down the steps of the imposing house. At least, he thought, he had made some headway, and he would meet the mysterious Mr Humbie.

MR HUMBIE

Back in Kingsferry, Kate continued to make progress. Now, though still weak, she was able to get up and sit by the fire and help with some of the household chores.

'Ye've been fair kind tae me,' she told Eliza one day. 'You and Miss Maggie and Miss Stuart. The minister has been here, too. He brocht some honey frae his ain bees,' she added.

'We're glad to see you recovered,' Eliza said, smiling.

'There's maybe not much we can dae for ye,' Kate said. 'Except for Robbie—he can aye run messages—when he's not at the school. And he doesna attend school much. The minister was trying to get him to go, but Robbie wad sooner be down the harbour, helping at the boats. He's set on going to sea, like his faither.' She sighed. 'And it's a dangerous life.'

Eliza did not know what to say, but she stretched out a hand and patted Kate consolingly on the arm.

'There's plenty time yet before he is big enough.'

On the way home with Catriona, she felt unusually down in spirits. Kate was recovering, the fever had gone, and she would soon regain her strength. Maggie had become a good friend and there was always cheerful company at the manse. But somehow the savour had gone out of life. Why was that? It couldn't be anything to do with Jamie's departure. No, that was nonsense. He was simply a good friend, and in any case, he belonged to Catriona. Hadn't she seen the kindly way he helped her, his concern for her welfare?

Besides, there was Catriona herself. She was these days slightly remote, though she had worked willingly in nursing Kate, and had treated the sick woman with great gentleness and kindness, but now she had returned to her usual reserved manner. Eliza doubted whether they would ever be really close.

Her mind raced ahead. Surely this was a sign of being in love, this detachment from the world? She did not really know, as most of her knowledge was taken from novels, but it seemed to her very likely that she was head over heels in love with Jamie.

She sighed. She had become fond of Catriona, especially since she knew of her background, but, oh, what a fortunate girl Catriona would be to be wooed by someone like Jamie.

Meantime, she tried to be practical. Why did Jamie not get in touch? He had promised. Eliza knew that the King's visit was happening very soon, but surely Jamie had by now some clue about the plans to bring Catriona to Edinburgh?

Maggie tried to reassure her.

'We can trust Jamie,' she said. 'I am sure there will be news very soon.'

*   *   *

In Edinburgh that Sunday evening, Jamie glanced in the looking-glass to make sure that his stock was properly tied. He brushed the shoulders of his coat, and took up his tall hat.

He wished that the evening was over, but he knew that this was his best chance of meeting the mysterious Mr Humbie.

At the big house in Charlotte Square, there was a buzz of activity. Carriages and sedan chairs drew up at the open door, and from inside the glow of dozens of candles spread out into the dusk.

Jamie paused, watching a small group of people getting out of their carriages, the ladies in elegant silks, clutching new Paisley shawls around their shoulders, like a flock of bright humming birds.

Indoors flunkeys bowed and escorted the guests to the first floor, where the sparkle of the magnificent candelabra lit up the intricate plaster cornices, and the portraits of solemn, long-dead ancestors, who seemed to gaze down on the chattering groups of guests with disapproving stares.

'Ah, there you are!' Aunt Bess was magnificently dressed for the occasion. She wore a gown of deep crimson velvet with a matching turban. Turbans were very much in fashion and Aunt Bess was determined to show that she was one of Edinburgh's leaders when it came to displaying the latest styles. She broke off from greeting another guest and took Jamie by the arm.

'There are some young ladies I would like you to meet.'

Jamie felt a little sorry for the two girls who were standing by the door, though they were stylishly dressed in silk and satin, with feathered headdresses. Both looked a little bewildered by the sparkle of the occasion. Introduced by Aunt Bess, he bowed, and asked if he might fetch them a glass of punch.

'Oh, yes, please,' the younger girl said eagerly. 'We know no-one here, as you may have gathered, and have only just arrived.'

Jamie waved to a passing waiter.

'So, you have come to Edinburgh for this occasion,' he said.

'We have travelled from Perthshire,' the first said. 'And it is so exciting. We have rooms with a balcony on Picardy Street and we expect to have a splendid view of the procession.'

'I have never seen quite so many Highlanders,' the other said. 'It makes you wonder whether there are any left in the Highlands.'

'But think of the benefit to the tailors,' Jamie said. 'It seems that everyone in

Edinburgh wants to wear the kilt.'

'And the dressmakers and the mantua makers,' the older sister put in. 'We ourselves are a benefit to trade in the city.' She laughed, and Jamie thought what a lively, attractive pair of sisters they were.

Jamie was not accustomed to grand social occasions, so he was rather at a loss for anything more to say. He glanced around the room, at the glow of the candles, the splendour of the guests and the magnificence of the pictures and furniture. He wished he was not alone.

Oh, how she would enjoy this, he thought. But then his attention was caught by a tall figure, all in black, who paused in the doorway and seemed to scan the company with a disapproving look. Could it be, he wondered, that this was the lawyer he had come to meet?

'You are absent, sir.' One of the girls tapped him playfully on the arm with her ivory fan.

'I do apologise.' Jamie was contrite. 'A momentary absence of mind only, I assure you.' But it was with relief that he saw a fair-haired young man with an outdoors complexion cross the floor and approach the two girls.

'It is good to see you here.' He beamed at them. 'I did not know you were coming to Edinburgh.'

'How could you not?' the older girl said. 'We have talked of nothing else for some months. We had thought the whole country would know of our expedition.' She laughed at him

'You must forgive me,' he said. 'I have been away.'

'We are near neighbours in Perthshire,' the young woman explained to Jamie. 'And it is good to find a familiar face in this throng.'

After a few minutes Jamie excused himself politely.

'Perhaps I may have the pleasure of meeting you again?' Out of the corner of his eye he could see the gaunt black figure approaching the receiving line and he made his way cautiously towards his aunt, who was still greeting friends and acquaintances. There was no sign of his uncle, he thought with a grin, and Jamie guessed that he was in his library, among his books, with a pipe and a dram of whisky, quite content.

'Jamie!' Heads turned as Bess accosted her nephew. 'Here is the gentleman I want you to meet, Mr Humbie.' She greeted the tall, silent figure. 'How good of you to grace with your presence my little gathering. Now you must meet my nephew, James Grieve, a young lawyer of quite exceptional promise. I say this as his aunt, but I am not the only one to be sure that he is destined for great things.' She paused for a moment to draw breath, then said, 'I feel sure you will have a great deal to talk about.'

Mr Humbie raised his eyebrows and said stiffly, 'I am honoured to be invited to your gathering, madam. And it is a pleasure to meet your nephew.' He turned to Jamie.

'Shall we withdraw to a quieter corner,' the lawyer said, 'and enjoy a glass of wine, perhaps?'

Once they were seated in an alcove, the lawyer fixed his gaze on Jamie, who felt that he was being very closely scrutinised.

'Tell me . . .' The lawyer leaned forward and drummed his long fingers on a little table, '. . . where do you come from?'

Jamie explained.

'I work in Edinburgh, but my home is in Kingsferry.'

'Kingsferry?' The lawyer gave a low whistle. 'And you visit there?'

'I have only just returned, sir,' Jamie said. 'I was convalescing there.'

'Indeed. I hope you are quite recovered.'

'Thank you, sir. I am quite well again.'

There was a pause.

'I imagine,' the lawyer said, 'that you do not, as yet, earn a great deal.' His sharp eyes had taken in Jamie's coat, which was brushed but hardly new. His stock, too, was freshly laundered, but it was not in the height of fashion.

'I do well enough, sir,' Jamie replied a little stiffly. He wondered what the lawyer was proposing.

115

'I might,' Humbie said slowly, 'I might be able to put some work your way.' He coughed, putting his hand to his mouth. 'I am sure you are not averse to earning a little extra. Surely for a young lawyer, making his way, dealing with pleas and such like cannot be very rewarding. I know only too well how difficult it can be. So perhaps I can help by offering you some extra work?' He gave a smile that exposed his yellowing teeth, and made him look, so Jamie thought, a little like some wild animal. A fox, perhaps.

'That depends, sir.'

'Indeed. On what, may I ask?'

'Whether the work offered is, may I say, honest.' Jamie wondered if he had offended this strange man. But what if he had? He was not obliged to accept any man's shilling.

To his surprise, the lawyer gave another smile, which was in itself off-putting.

'Ah, the young man has principles, has he? Very good.' He paused for a moment or two, still looking directly at Jamie.

'I think,' he said slowly, 'that you and I should talk further. And here, at your good aunt's soirée, is not the best of times. Perhaps I could suggest that you come to my offices tomorrow.' He scribbled a note, and handed it to Jamie. 'And you and I will have a most fruitful discussion.'

He raised his glass.

'A toast.' He moved the glass over the

116

finger bowl on the table. 'To the King.' Then he whispered under his breath so Jamie could only just make it out. 'Over the water.'

As Jamie made his way home that evening, his thoughts were confused. He would keep the appointment, of course he would. There was something very strange about Humbie. He had heard of the man and knew that he had been involved in some dubious dealings. And that toast? Had he heard right? Had the lawyer really said, 'to the King over the water'? In which case, was he toasting not George IV, at this moment sailing towards Leith, but the Jacobite Prince, Charles Edward Stuart, now dead these many years, but still very much in the minds and hearts of his supporters.

Was Mr Humbie a secret Jacobite, and what did he want with Jamie?

A PROPOSITION

As Jamie climbed the stairs to the lawyer's office the following day, he saw that clearly very little money had been spent on furnishing. The carpet was worn and frayed, and the curtains hanging at the window were torn and dirty. The lawyer himself was seated at his desk, peering through his spectacles at a sheaf of papers. Hesitantly, Jamie knocked at the door.

'You wished to see me, sir?'

'Indeed I did.' The lawyer flung down the sheaf of papers and got to his feet. 'Come in, come in!' He ushered Jamie to a chair, and Jamie wondered, a little uneasily, what was the reason for this lavish welcome.

'Well!' The lawyer sat down again and regarded Jamie with a smile which Jamie felt made him look even more sinister.

'You have told me a little about your circumstances,' Humbie said. 'I think you said you come from Kingsferry.'

Jamie nodded.

'And your father is minister of the local church. That is so? And you have a sister living at home? Thus, I gather from that . . .' The lawyer leaned back, putting the tips of his fingers together, '. . . that there is not a great deal of money in your family. Apart from your aunt.'

Jamie said hastily, 'I am independent of my aunt, sir.'

'Quite so, quite so.' The lawyer smiled again. 'I gather that you support, as best you can, your father and sister.'

'As far as I can, sir.'

'Good, good.' He had an irritating habit of repeating phrases, Jamie thought. 'That is what I like to hear. A young man who wishes to make his own way in the world and support his family. But, I gather,' he went on, 'that you would not be averse to earning a little

118

extra. To supplement your income? I cannot imagine that your wage in your present post is a princely one.'

Come to the point, Jamie thought.

'I understand you have a proposition to put to me? As I said when we spoke yesterday, I will not countenance anything which is at all dubious.'

'Spoken like a son of the manse! Good, good.' The lawyer laid his hands, palms down, on the desk. 'When, last night, I gave the toast to the King over the water, you did not contradict me.'

'I thought it would be impolite, sir.'

'Ah. But you must be aware, are you not, that there are still those of us who are loyal to the Chevalier, who would wish to see a Stuart on the throne of Scotland. Those who are fiercely opposed to this English King, who is to be tricked out in tartan as King of Scots. Pah!'

Jamie was silent, and Humbie continued.

'For some time now, we have had loyal supporters, here and in France, who are eager to bring a Stuart to Scotland, and seat her on the throne at Holyrood.' He leaned back, looking closely at Jamie.

'Her?' Jamie said, knowing very well what was coming.

'Her, indeed!' The lawyer laughed. 'You may be aware that living in Kingsferry is a young lady, newly arrived from Belgium, who is the rightful heir to the throne. A Miss

Catriona Stuart, legitimate descendant of the Chevalier. The plan . . .' He leaned closer, and spoke in a low voice, though there was no-one around as far as Jamie could see, '. . . is that Miss Catriona Stuart shall be brought to Edinburgh ahead of the King's visit next week, and by the time wee Geordie arrives, she will be installed in Holyrood, there to be crowned as the rightful Queen of Scotland.'

The man must be mad, Jamie thought, noting the lawyer's glittering eyes and heightened colour.

'And how,' Jamie asked carefully, 'is this to be arranged? Perhaps Miss Stuart does not want to be Queen.'

'She has no choice,' Humbie said coldly. 'It is all planned. She will sail from Kingsferry to Leith and be collected there by coach and then taken to Holyrood. It is a pity,' he added, 'that she cannot be driven through the streets to the cheers of the crowds. There will be many waiting there and on Calton Hill, to acclaim wee Geordie. But we do not wish to start a riot.'

'And what is it that you wish me to do?'

The lawyer did not seem to notice the steely note in Jamie's voice.

'You will be there on the quay at Leith when the *Clementina* docks. You will help the young lady into the carriage and drive with her to Holyrood. That is all.'

'Do you propose I should act alone?'

120

'And why not?' the lawyer said. 'My henchman, a loyal Jacobite, is in Kingsferry at this moment. He is guarding the young lady and making sure she comes to no harm. When the moment comes, she will board the fishing vessel, which will not attract attention among so many boats, and sail for Leith.'

'And what,' Jamie went on dangerously, 'is there of profit to me?'

In reply, the lawyer reached into a drawer of his desk and brought out a bag of sovereigns.

'There!' he said. 'That's your answer.' He flung the bag on the desk.

'Go on, man, take it!'

In reply, Jamie rose and reached across the desk, grabbing Humbie by the points of his collar.

'Keep your money!' he said angrily. 'Do you think I am to be bought?' His voice trembled. 'Do you think I would connive in the abduction of an innocent young woman? Do you think I would have any part in this traitorous scheme?'

He drew a deep breath.

'If that is the case, you have misjudged me.'

The lawyer shook himself free.

'I thought,' he said in his high, reedy voice, 'that you were one of us. One of the Jacobites.'

I was a fool to come here, Jamie thought. But now at least I know what are his plans.

Humbie huddled down in his chair.

'I thought,' he protested, 'that you would be willing to play a part for the great glory of your country. I had you marked out as a simple young man from the country, confident, able to carry himself, but somewhat in need of money. But it seems I was wrong.'

'Indeed you were.'

Jamie turned to go.

'Good day, sir.'

As he slammed the door behind him, Jamie heard the lawyer call out, 'Never speak of this. You would do well to keep it secret.'

Jamie hurried downstairs. His mind was in a whirl and he knew, only too well, that decisions had to be made quickly. He knew, too, that Humbie would act immediately. He would want to bring Catriona to Edinburgh without delay. And Jamie was aware that he himself was not safe. He cursed himself for a hasty reaction. Why could he not have played for time, why had he not pretended that he might just have considered the lawyer's proposition?

The first thing, he knew, was to get word urgently to Eliza. She must make sure that Catriona was safe, that she was away from danger by the time the *Clementina* sailed for Leith.

There was no time to lose.

GRAVE DANGER

Back in Kingsferry, the housekeeper raised her head from the table and groaned. In her befuddled state she had not heard the door open. Now the man in black stood over her.

'A fine wardress you are!' he growled. 'Here you were, charged with keeping the young lady under guard, and what happens?'

'Eh?' She looked up at him blearily.

He picked up an empty bottle of gin, and flung it from him with an expression of disgust.

'I didna ken,' she began.

'You kent fine,' he said. 'You were supposed to keep close watch on her, but did you? She's been all over the place. At a fisherman's wee hoose in the wynd, up at the manse, in the shops. How's that for keeping close watch?' He went on. 'From now you'll watch her every moment of the day. There's to be no going out and in, visiting here and there. She's to be kept a prisoner, do you understand? And in a day or two she'll be fetched, and taken off to Leith.'

She looked at him blearily and nodded.

He grunted.

'And see you keep an eye on that ither wan, the lass frae Edinburgh. She's far ower sharp tae ma mind. I've strict instructions, she's tae be weel guarded.'

'I'll hae ma work cut out,' she grumbled.

Two days later, the eagerly awaited message from Jamie arrived. Maggie opened the envelope and scanned the contents hurriedly.

'At last!' she said. 'I knew that Jamie would not be idle.'

She took the letter to show to her father. He read it slowly then looked over his spectacles at Maggie.

'There is only one thing we can do, as far as I can see. We must offer a home to that poor child, Miss Catriona, for as long as she needs it.'

'I thought you would say that!' Maggie cried. 'How good you are! I will go right away to Shore House, but I'm afraid it will be difficult. That fearsome old woman is loath to let Catriona out of her sight.'

'However,' she added as she tied the strings of her bonnet, 'I will do what I can. And you are a dear, good father to welcome her to the manse.'

It was a fine morning as Maggie made her way down the hill. Today promised to be warm, and she wished, as she often did, that she had a light cotton dress for the summer days. But there were more important things to consider than dresses.

She knocked at the door of Shore House, noting that the knocker had not been polished and paint was flaking from the door. The windows, too, were grimy, the net curtains torn, and the whole place had the air of neglect.

She waited, tapping her foot impatiently, and then the door was flung open and the housekeeper appeared.

'So, what is it you're wanting?' The woman glared at Maggie.

Maggie made an effort to keep her temper.

'To speak with Miss Dunlop and Miss Stuart.'

'Ye canna come in.'

'I beg your pardon?' Maggie said in as chilling a tone as she could.

'I said, you're not to come in, and the twa lassies are no' tae get oot.'

'On whose authority?' Maggie faced the woman.

'That's naething tae dae wi' you,' the housekeeper spat. 'I've had my orders—you're not to get seeing them, and they're not tae gang visiting you and ither fowk.'

With that she slammed the door in Maggie's face.

Maggie stood, wondering what she should do. She looked up at the windows of the house and fancied she saw a hand draw aside the net curtain. So here was a pickle! She fingered the letter from Jamie in the pocket of her gown. How was she to get in touch with Eliza, and warn her?

Despondent, she turned and made her way back up the hill. She couldn't let Jamie down, she told herself firmly, and she couldn't possibly leave Catriona in that house where she was in danger, it seemed, every minute of the days ahead. She had thought the housekeeper was difficult, but now she understood. The woman was dangerous, too.

At the manse, her father was in his study, deep in his books. He looked up, keeping a finger in the volume to mark his place.

'Well, daughter? Did you see Miss Catriona?'

'I did not,' Maggie said grimly. She explained what had happened.

'Dear me,' the minister replied. The gentle expression was the fiercest he would ever allow himself.

'So what is there to be done?' Maggie cried. 'The house is like a fortress—there is no way in, front or back, because that gorgon guards the kitchen.'

'I will think of something,' the minister promised. He laid aside his book. 'Give me a little time.'

Maggie looked at him in despair. He was the kindest of fathers, but no-one could call him practical. She and Jamie had often laughed at his dreamy ways, how far removed he was from the concerns of everyday life. What could he possibly do to help? She could not see him springing into action.

Maggie, in a very bad temper, stamped off to the kitchen and spoke sharply to the maid who had done nothing towards preparing the vegetables for the dinner.

'Am I to do everything myself?' she scolded the girl.

Later that day, she saw her father wandering round his garden, and thought crossly how typical that was. He had never been a man who would act decisively in any crisis, and if this wasn't a crisis, what was? But there he wouldn't change, and there was no point in trying to make him any different.

When Mr Grieve came indoors, he was holding a bunch of white roses that he had gathered from the garden.

'Very suitable, I thought,' he said.

'For what?' Maggie was still cross.

He smiled at her, recognising that she had expected him to think of a solution to their problem.

'They are the variety known as the Jacobite rose,' he said. 'And I propose to send a bunch to Miss Catriona—and Miss Eliza, too—with the message from Jamie hidden among the blooms.'

'Well,' Maggie said thoughtfully, 'I suppose it would be one way to send a message, but how are you going to be allowed into Shore House?'

'We will send Robbie,' her father said placidly. 'If he cannot gain access, no-one can.'

When Robbie called at the manse for his weekly lesson in reading and writing, the

127

minister said kindly, 'Not today, my son. We have a more important task for you.'

Robbie's eyes widened. More important than reading and writing?

'You must take these roses to Miss Eliza,' Maggie told him. 'And be sure to give them to no-one else. Certainly not to the housekeeper.'

Robbie nodded. He had had several encounters with Mistress Kilbain, and had felt the rough edge of her tongue. 'Inside there is a message.' Maggie showed him the scrap of paper hidden among the stems. 'It is to tell Miss Eliza to bring Miss Catriona to the manse tomorrow night, without fail.

'But this is a secret,' she impressed on him. 'You must tell no-one.'

Robbie promised.

'I'll no' tell.'

'Good lad. Now,' Maggie wondered, 'there is the problem of how you get into the house.'

'Nae bother.' The boy winked at her. 'I ken the way in.'

'We are relying on you,' Maggie told him. 'And here, for your trouble, are a couple of bannocks.'

*   *   *

It was late morning, and Robbie had already been up early, helping one of the fishermen down at the harbour. The man had thrown him a few herring as reward. Normally Robbie

would have taken these home, but now he saw
the fish as a way into Shore House.

Carefully holding the bunch of roses, he
picked up the fish that he had left at the
back door of the manse, and made his way
down to Shore House. He had no idea of the
time, but from the smell of cooking coming
from the kitchen, he guessed that it was near
dinnertime.

He made his way up the narrow lane at the
side of the house, and cautiously pushed open
the kitchen door.

'Are ye there, missus?' he called out, seeing
that the kitchen was empty. There was a pot of
kail simmering on the stove. He took the lid
off the pot and sniffed appreciatively.

There was still no sign of the housekeeper,
so he took the herring and the bunch of roses
and made his way along the passage. He had
never been in the dining-room, but could hear
the sound of voices, so guessed that the two
young ladies must be at their dinner.

'Hey, missus!' He peered round the door.

'Michty!' The housekeeper, in the act of
serving the soup, dropped the ladle. 'What do
you want? Ye've nae business here.'

'There was naebody in the kitchen so I cam
through,' Robbie said, quite unperturbed.

'Well, ye can just tak yourself aff again,' the
housekeeper told him. 'The very idea!'

Eliza and Catriona looked at him, surprised,
Eliza with an expression of dawning hope.

'I brocht ye some herring,' Robbie said.

'Well, ye can just leave them on the kitchen table and be on your way again. And whit's this?' She looked suspiciously at Robbie, who was clutching the bunch of roses.

'They're for Miss Eliza,' he said. 'From the minister.'

'How kind of him,' Eliza murmured. 'They're his special white roses—the Jacobite rose, he told me.'

'He's written you a message,' Robbie said in a low voice. They exchanged glances, and then Eliza delved into the bunch and came out with a slip of paper.

She pretended to read it out.

'I thought you might like these—the Jacobite rose. They are at their best just now.'

'Jacobite roses, eh?' The housekeeper allowed herself a small smile. 'Well, I suppose there's nae herm in the minister sending a flooer.'

Eliza drew a deep breath.

'And such a kind message. You may—' she hesitated, 'you may read it if you wish.'

Mistress Kilbain sniffed.

'Ye ken fine I canna read and write.'

'Such a pity,' Eliza said, looking directly at the woman.

'Weel,' the housekeeper began, 'I've never felt the lack o't.' She turned to Robbie. 'Take they smelly fish oot o' ma dining-room.'

When Robbie had gone and the

130

housekeeper had returned to the kitchen, Eliza folded the paper and tucked it into the bodice of her dress.

Then she rose and closed the door firmly.

Catriona laid down her spoon.

'So—the message? What did it say?'

'It said,' Eliza knew the message by heart, 'Bring Catriona to the manse tonight. She is in grave danger.'

Eliza threw down her napkin.

'We mustn't waste any time. Tonight, he says. And there are plans to be made. I knew,' she added with a smile, 'I knew Jamie wouldn't let us down. I would trust him with my life—and with yours.'

A PLACE OF SAFETY

The days were sunlit and, on these summer evenings, it was late before the sun went down and became dark. All through the afternoon and evening, Eliza was planning the best way to get Catriona out of Shore House and up to the manse.

'We shall need only a simple meal,' she told the housekeeper, 'after that good dinner. Bannocks and cheese, perhaps?'

'Aye, right.'

Eliza went upstairs and knocked at the door of Catriona's room.

'I think we must decide,' she said, 'what you are to wear.' She opened the wardrobe door and looked through the dresses that hung there. There was a fine wool dress embroidered with flowers, a creamy satin, a pale pink silk.

'No,' she said thoughtfully, 'these are too fine. Anyone watching would recognise you right away. You must look plain and inconspicuous.'

'I am, how do you say, content to leave those clothes behind,' Catriona said. 'They were given to me. In the convent I wore only plain dresses. They are more suitable.'

Eliza fingered the silk dresses and fine wool shawls.

'I fear there is nothing really suitable here.'

'Then why do we not change clothes?' Catriona asked.

'What a good idea!'

Neither of the girls had much appetite for the cheese and bannocks that the housekeeper laid before them.

'Try to eat a little,' Eliza urged Catriona. 'Or it will look suspicious.'

The evening seemed to pass with exasperating slowness. Oh, if only it would get dark, Eliza thought impatiently.

At last it was time to go. But first, Eliza slipped downstairs to the kitchen. She had prepared an excuse of wanting a drink of buttermilk if the housekeeper should still be awake and alert.

But they were in luck. As soon as Eliza pushed open the kitchen door, she heard the sound of deep snoring. Mistress Kilbain was slumped back in her chair beside the fire, her mouth wide open, and quite oblivious of anything going on. The pots had not been cleared from the table, but there was a bottle of gin by her side, and she had clearly wasted no time before settling for the night.

Eliza crept upstairs again.

'Now, it is time,' she whispered, and the girls made their way downstairs; Catriona, clutching her valise, and wearing Eliza's rough wool cloak, Eliza in the cloak of blue velvet.

'Hurry,' Eliza whispered as they made their way out into the lane.

She grasped Catriona by the arm and pulled her back into the shadows as a figure appeared round the corner.

'Stay still,' she ordered. Then she laughed quietly. 'Oh, it is you, Robbie!' she said as the boy appeared from the shadows.

'The minister said I was to look after you.'

'We are grateful,' Eliza said. 'Now let's not waste time.'

She was thankful when they arrived safely at the manse, although for most of the way she had been glancing fearfully over her shoulder.

'Here you are!' Maggie opened the door wide. 'I'm sure I am glad to see you.'

Her father appeared and greeted Catriona

warmly. 'You can be certain you will be safe here,' he told her, and Maggie put her arms round the girl.

'It is very kind of you,' Catriona said, her voice near breaking. 'I do not know what I would have done without my good friends.'

'Nonsense! We are glad to have you.'

Robbie handed over Catriona's valise.

'I'll be away, missus. The captain's coming the night.'

'Then you won't want to miss him.' Maggie smiled at the boy. 'He's a grand storyteller, the captain.'

'They're not stories, they're true!' the boy protested.

'Of course,' Maggie said hastily. She knew that the bluff, slow-spoken captain was already a hero to young Robbie.

'Come away in,' she told Catriona. 'And you, too, Eliza. Young Isa's been baking today so you'll stay and take something with us.'

Eliza shook her head.

'I must go back. Mistress Kilbain was sound asleep when we left, but she may wake up and . . .'

Maggie put a hand on her friend's arm.

'Oh, you will be careful, won't you? Please don't run any risks. And what will you tell her about Catriona?'

'Perhaps I could say she has a chill and is having an early night?' Eliza suggested. She knew that the housekeeper was afraid of

134

illness, and besides, she would not want the extra work of looking after an invalid. 'And tomorrow I will think of something else.'

'Tomorrow,' Maggie said, 'there is sure to be more news from Jamie.'

'You are very good, both of you.' Eliza turned to Maggie and the minister. 'To take in a stranger and shelter her in your home.'

The minister smiled.

'Oh, this manse has been a sanctuary before now,' he said. 'During the Napoleonic Wars, the press gang scoured the East Neuk of Fife. They raided homes all along the coast, recruiting men for the Navy. Sometimes,' he added, 'the men were away for years, and were not even allowed to say farewell to their loved ones. But here, in the manse, there is a secret room where men were hidden, to remain in safety until the press gang had gone.'

'And is the room still here?' Eliza asked.

The minister smiled knowingly.

'Yes, and ready for the shelter of any soul in danger.'

'I know Catriona will be safe with you.'

'And I will pray for your safety, my child,' he said, and Eliza felt comforted.

As she made her way down the hill towards Shore House, Eliza felt overwhelmingly lonely. Usually she was of an optimistic nature, but now she felt downcast, and ever so slightly afraid.

Don't be so foolish, she told herself. There

was no danger now to Catriona, who would be protected and cared for at the manse. The minister might be remote, he might live in a world far from everyday concerns, but she was perfectly sure that he would be strong and courageous in the face of danger. And she felt reassured that he would be equally concerned for her safety.

No, that was not the reason she felt so out of sorts. It was because she had left behind a warm, loving household, where people cared for one another. And no-one, she thought in a rare spasm of self-pity, no-one cared for her. She sighed. Jamie would never care for her. He was simply Maggie's brother and it was high time she stopped having romantic daydreams about him. Besides, she was almost certain that he was in love with Catriona.

With a heavy heart, she opened the door of Shore House and went inside.

Indoors it was very quiet. There was no sound from the kitchen. Without Catriona's presence the house seemed unusually silent, though Catriona did not talk a great deal. Still, she was a pleasant companion, and it was comforting to have someone of Eliza's own age around.

Eliza could not bear the oppressive nature of the house a moment longer; the heavy furniture, the tattered curtains, the musty smell that seemed to pervade every corner.

She longed to be outdoors, to breathe the

salty air, to hear the murmur of the waves against the sea wall, to watch the stars in the night sky, and to see the lights of the fishing boats distantly across the Firth.

She turned and made her way out of the house, enjoying the feel of the cool night air and wrapping the dark blue cloak comfortingly around her. How luxurious it felt, the velvet material, as she pulled the hood up.

As she leaned her elbows on the sea wall, Eliza thought of all that had happened since she first rang the bell of Shore House. Her growing friendship with Catriona, the pleasant companionship of Maggie and the minister, meeting Robbie and his family. But here she refused to dwell on thoughts of Jamie.

And that was an end of it. Nothing more would happen, she felt certain. Whatever plot Jamie had unmasked in Edinburgh, Eliza was sure she and Catriona would now be perfectly safe in Kingsferry.

Suddenly she heard swift steps behind her. Before she had time to realise what was happening, she was seized by rough hands, her arms pinioned behind her back. She tried to cry out, and a grimy hand was clamped over her mouth.

'Wheesht!' a voice growled in her ear.

She tried to struggle free, but her captor was too strong. She was swept off her feet and she realised she was being carried away from Shore House, down towards the harbour. She tried to kick out at the man, but it was no use.

'Bide still,' he said in her ear. 'Or it'll be worse for you.'

Now Eliza felt nauseous with fear. Her mind in a whirl, she knew only one thing. That she must stay awake and alert—that she must not give in.

MISTAKEN IDENTITY

The next thing Eliza knew, a grimy rag was bound over her eyes. She struggled, without success, and was only aware that they were on the cobbles that led down to the quay. She had been to the harbour often enough, and guessed that she was to be taken prisoner on a fishing boat.

Eliza tried to remove the blindfold, but one of the men had tied her hands behind her back. A moment later she was flung roughly on to a boat. She knew from the strong smell of fish that it must be one of those moored in the harbour. And then she was pushed on to a narrow bunk, both hands so tightly tied that she could not move.

She tried to call out, but a voice told her, 'It's nae use. They'll no hear ye.' A second man laughed unpleasantly.

Then there was a rattle of chains, a splash, and shouts. It was no use now. They had set sail for Leith, she hoped. Oh, pray heaven, it might be Leith. Then there was some chance of escape once she was in the city. She lay, not moving, wondering what would happen to her. But, if by some change of plan, the boat was sailing for the Low Countries, she knew she could not survive the voyage.

She knew from the way the little boat rose and fell with the waves that they must be approaching open sea. She shuddered, remembering the steam packet on the way to Inverkeithing and the way the wind had driven her below decks. But this was August! Surely the sea should be calm.

She lay very still, putting up a prayer that she would at least see the other side.

Up on deck she could hear voices, and she strained to listen.

'I dinna like this. She's only a bit lass.'

She recognised this voice. It sounded like the man who had grabbed her at Shore House.

'Ye're being weel paid,' a second voice said, gruffer than the first. 'It doesna matter if you like it or no'.'

There was a pause, then the first man said, 'When we dock, that's the job done?'

'Aye,' the second man agreed. 'There's a coach waiting tae tak the lass tae Holyrood.'

'Whit fur?'

'Ye're nae wise,' the second said, a touch of exasperation in his voice. 'D'ye no' ken wha she is? She's the great granddaughter of the Bonnie Prince, and the rightful Queen o' Scotland.'

'Save us!' The first spoke in awed tones. 'Is that richt?'

'I wadna be makin' it up.' The second man sounded even more exasperated. 'I was telt by yon man the lawyer sent.'

'Him that walks aboot the toon dressed in black? I took him for a preacher.'

'Naw, he's a spy. So by the time wee Geordie steps ashore, the lass will be sat in Holyrood Palace.'

'But,' the first man protested, 'there's sure tae be hundred o' polis.'

'Mebbe,' the second man agreed, 'but there's a wheen o' Chairlie's Jacobites in Edinburgh— in Fife, too, there's some o' them in Crail. Fowk hae lang memories. There's plenty fowk dinna want wee Geordie tae be King o' Scots.'

Eliza gasped. So that was it! They'd planned right from the beginning to kidnap Catriona, and to keep her safely out of sight until the King's visit, then to bring her to Holyrood. Poor Catriona! She clearly had no idea of what would happen to her.

No wonder the man in black had kept such a close watch.

Eliza's mind raced ahead. What will happen to me?

These were paid assassins. She was afraid that they would not hesitate to kill her once they found out that the whole scheme had foundered. After all, she had no relatives, no friends, except . . . She wondered where Jamie was. Events had gathered pace, everything had happened so quickly. He would not know, she thought, that Catriona was safe in the manse.

She tried to struggle up from the narrow bunk, but then another wave came roaring in, battering the frail little boat, which seemed to be tossed around as if made of paper.

'I'll awa doon below and see the lass is a' richt,' the first man said.

'And why should she no' be?' Eliza could hear over the drumming of the waves the voice of the second man.

'I'm no' happy about this,' the first repeated. 'Ye ken that weemen are no' allowed on fishing boats.'

The second man snorted.

'Ye're just superstitious. And if anyone were to see her, they'd no speak o't. It wad bring bad luck.' He laughed. 'Just as weel we didna meet the minister on the way. We'd have had to turn back.'

'I thocht ye said ye werena superstitious.'

'It's weel kent,' the other sailor began, 'that ministers bring bad luck to the fishing.' He went on. 'I'll tak a turn at the wheel. If ye're gaun tae see to the lass, dinna be lang aboot it. My,' he said, 'there's a richt swell on. Ah doot his Majesty will no' be able tae land at Leith.' He snorted. 'I'm thinking he'll no' be much of a sailor, wee Geordie.'

Eliza lay as still as she could, pretending to be asleep. How long would this go on, she wondered, and what would happen when they reached Leith. But, she comforted herself, at least they were bound for Leith, and she need not fear a dreadful voyage over the North Sea.

The man who had come to check on her leaned over. Eliza suffered inwardly and tried not to wrinkle up her nose. How he smelled! A reek of stale whisky and unwashed clothes, mixed with the smell of tar and fish. She tried hard not to breathe in, and was thankful when he turned aside and climbed back on deck.

The swell, and the rise and fall of the boat, seemed to last for hours. Eliza tried hard to fight the nausea that arose in her as each wave reached its crest. She tried desperately to think of other matters, but it was of little use. With her hands tied behind her back she could not grasp the sides of the bunk, and she was tossed backwards and forwards like a parcel.

When would they remove the blindfold, Eliza wondered. Then suddenly she was aware that the sea was at last becoming calmer. They must be nearing port. She winced a little as she tried to move her legs in the cramped space.

'We're near there,' she heard one man say. 'Ahead o' time. So we'll moor here till the carriage turns up.'

'See the crowds!' she heard the other say. 'They're a' waiting for the King.'

'More fool them,' the first man growled. 'The King'll no' be here for a whilie. The weather's ower bad for His Majesty to land. Still, it's fine for us. They'll no' notice onything oot o' the ordinary.'

What was going to happen to her, Eliza wondered with a shiver. Sooner or later, they would realise that she was not Catriona.

Suddenly, it seemed, everything happened at once. She could hear the sounds of shouts, the thud of feet jumping on the deck, the boat being tied up. Thankfully, she realised that at least this part of the ordeal was over.

Both men stumbled down into the cabin.

'That's it then,' the second said. 'Our job's done. We've only got to wait for the carriage. Mr Humbie said it would be here.'

Rough hands dragged Eliza to her feet. She tried to wrap the blue cloak around her and struggled to free herself from the blindfold.

'Bide there,' the second man told her roughly. And he turned back the hood of the cloak.

He gazed down on Eliza with an expression she could not at first understand. Fear? Horror?

Then he swung round and grasped the first sailor by the throat.

'Ye donnert fool!' he growled. 'Ye blitherin'dolt!'

The first struggled in his grasp and gazed at him, not understanding.

143

'See what you've done!' He stared at Eliza, at her light brown hair, now lank, uncurled, and her pale cheeks.

'Whit's that?' The first wriggled free.

'Ye've ta'en the wrang lass!'

'Well,' the first said with an air of injured innocence, 'hoo was I tae ken?'

'Miss Stuart has red hair. And this lass looks naethin like her. This is no' her.'

Eliza shuddered. What would happen to her now?

'I wasna telt.' The first man tried to justify himself. 'I was telt a blue cloak, and that was richt.'

'But ye didna hae the mense tae look at her. Ye were ower busy drinkin'wi' the auld woman at the hoose.' The second man groaned. He was silent for a moment, staring at Eliza. Then he said, 'I'll tell you. We'll say naething, ye understaun'?' He seized the other man by the arm. 'Once she's on that carriage, we'll get awa. Naebody will ken.'

'Fowk will ken,' the first objected.

'No' if we dinna blab,' the second sailor persisted. 'Ye'll keep yer mooth shut, understaun'? Keep the blindfold on her. If onybody guesses, we're for the jail. So we say naething.'

At that moment, Eliza realised that the boat had moored at the quay. She could hear the sound of thudding feet on the deck, the sound of shouting and curses. Then there was what

144

seemed like a scuffle on the quay, and angry voices.

'Get hold of her,' the first man ordered. He picked up Eliza and bent over her.

'Ye'll be a' richt,' he whispered. 'Ye'll be safe enough.' Despite the smell of stale whisky and the reek of fish from his clothing, Eliza felt oddly reassured. If only she could see what was happening. She struggled, trying to see through the blindfold.

But then his strong hands grasped her and she was lifted roughly from the narrow bunk. He untied the bonds that had bound her hands and feet.

'You're a' richt noo,' he muttered. 'Just bide there.' He clambered up the ladder on to the deck and was gone. Eliza breathed in the cool night air.

She could hear the clatter of hooves, the sound of a horse whinnying. Eliza tried to move her hands, but her wrists were sore and chafed and she could not stretch to untie the blindfold. Oh, what was going to happen, she thought in a sudden fit of panic. Would they leave her here? Would no-one know that she was a prisoner on the boat? Would they just abandon her?

Then there were more shouts.

'She's here!' a voice she thought she recognised shouted. A sturdy dark-clad figure leapt on to the deck. He clattered down into the cabin and gathered Eliza into his arms.

Gently he lifted her from the bunk where she lay, and removed the blindfold.

'You're quite safe now,' he said.

Bewildered, but filled with joy and relief, Eliza looked up at him.

'Oh, Jamie,' she said.

A CHANGE IN FORTUNE

'Don't be afraid,' Jamie said. 'You're all right now. Perfectly safe.'

He untied the bonds, and rubbed her wrists where the ropes had cut. Then he carried her to a carriage that was waiting on the quayside.

'I'll explain everything later,' he told her, and gave a quick word to the coachman.

The coach trundled from the quay as Eliza, bewildered by the rapid turn of events, peered in astonishment out of the window at the crowds which lined the banks of the harbour.

'They're waiting for the King's arrival,' Jamie said. 'But depending on the weather, he might not be here today.'

'But how did you know? And what about Catriona? And where are we going?' Eliza asked, her questions tumbling out one after another. She was confused by how quickly everything had happened. How did Jamie know she was on the *Clementina*?

'All in good time,' Jamie said. 'Things have

146

moved swiftly, and there was a message from a Norwegian captain that there was a strange fishing boat in the harbour at Kingsferry. He found out that she was due to sail to Leith yesterday evening, so we knew they planned to have Catriona on board?'

'But she is safe. At the manse,' Eliza interrupted.

'Thanks to you.'

'But how did you know I was to be on board?'

'It was a guess,' Jamie admitted. 'But I knew that they would not sail without Catriona, or someone very like her. The kidnappers would've been clapped in irons if they had arrived with no cargo.'

'I was afraid,' Eliza admitted, 'for a little time. But I knew I had only to hold on until we arrived at Leith.'

'You are indeed brave,' Jamie told her admiringly. 'And you have helped to foil a very dangerous plot. Now King George can land safely at Leith and the visit to Edinburgh will go ahead without any calamity. All the pageants and fireworks, balls and levees will proceed and no-one will be any the wiser that a Jacobite plot might have succeeded.'

'You must tell me everything that happened.' Eliza felt cold and damp and she shivered in the early morning mist.

'First,' Jamie said, 'you must have a hot meal and dry clothes or you will take a fever.'

'Where are we going?' Eliza's teeth chattered. Now that she was safe, she was beginning to feel the full horror of the night's events.

'To my aunt Bess. She lives in Charlotte Square. She will surely welcome you.' As he said this, Jamie was not at all sure of his aunt's welcome. To turn up at the door with a strange young woman—wet, bedraggled and with no luggage at all—he could well imagine his aunt's reaction. But there was nowhere else.

'My aunt and uncle have a large house,' he said. 'I am sure she will be happy to have you stay there.'

He spoke confidently, but looking at Eliza, damp, and dishevelled, and clearly still upset by her ordeal, he decided he must risk Aunt Bess's displeasure.

When they reached the tall, three-storeyed house, he helped Eliza out of the carriage, then ran up the steps and rang the bell.

'Is your mistress at home?' he asked.

The little parlour maid looked astonished at the sight of Eliza standing on the pavement, looking forlorn.

'Yes, sir,' she mumbled.

'You need not announce us. We will go right into the drawing-room. I know where it is.'

He grasped Eliza's hand and led her up the stairs.

'Don't be alarmed,' he told her. 'My aunt's

bark is worse than her bite. She has quite a kind heart underneath,' he added a little doubtfully.

'I am not afraid.' Eliza's spirits were recovering. 'Remember I was used to old Miss Gregory and her sharp tongue.'

'Of course,' Jamie smiled at her.

In the drawing-room, lying on the sofa, was Rosa, Jamie's cousin. Heavily pregnant, and very bored, she was idly flicking a fan backwards and forwards. When she saw Jamie, she sat up, her eyes sparkling.

'Cousin James! Where have you come from?' She peered a little short-sightedly at Eliza, who blushed and looked somewhat disconcerted.

'This is Miss Eliza Dunlop,' James said. 'My cousin, Mrs Rosa Macfadzean. I hope that my aunt will allow Miss Dunlop to stay for a few days.'

Rosa was clearly agog to know where Eliza had come from.

'Before you expire with curiosity,' Jamie said with a smile, 'I will tell you. There had been a plot,' he began.

Rosa shifted uncomfortably on the sofa, and prepared to listen.

Jamie began his account.

'So,' he said at last, 'after a most distressing voyage, Miss Eliza arrived at Leith this morning. I happened to be there,' he added casually.

149

Rosa rocked with laughter. She produced a lace-edged handkerchief from her reticule and mopped her eyes.

'How very amusing!' She gasped. 'It is just like a story—a romance.'

'There is no romance between your cousin and me!' Eliza broke in hastily.

'Really?' Rosa smiled. 'Then he is remiss, this cousin of mine. In all good novels the hero rescues a maiden in distress and immediately falls in love with her.'

Jamie, frowning a little, said, 'Well, as to that, I have told you what happened, and there are several Edinburgh burghers, including my aunt's friend and lawyer, Mr Humbie, who has been arrested and charged with sedition.'

'Dear me! If I were not in this condition,' she said, 'I should gladly introduce Miss Dunlop into Edinburgh society. It is a most exciting story.'

'What story?'

Jamie whirled round at the sound of his aunt's voice.

'No story, I assure you, Aunt. It is all perfectly true.'

His aunt gazed around the small group.

'And what, pray, has been happening? Will someone have the goodness to tell me?'

'Oh, Mama,' Rosa said. 'Such an adventure—and what extraordinary events!'

'Be quiet,' her mother admonished. 'You know it is unwise to become so agitated in your condition.' She shook her head at Rosa.

'Madam,' Jamie interrupted. 'Please hear me.'

Eliza, who was becoming more embarrassed every minute, sat down on a chair covered in fine brocade then, realising that her skirts were damp and grubby, leapt up again.

'Very well,' Aunt Bess said, settling herself in a wing chair by the fireside.

'Madam,' Jamie began again. 'I have come to ask if you will offer a few days' shelter to this young lady, who, as you can see, is in a state of considerable distress. Knowing your great generosity and your unfailing kindness to anyone in trouble, I felt I should come first to you.'

Jamie hurried on. He took a deep breath and began the tale. By now he was aware that he would probably have to tell it many times in the days ahead.

'So who is this young lady?' his aunt said when he had finished.

'A most respectable person,' Jamie assured her. 'She was companion to Miss Gregory, who lived in Heriot Row, and was with her until that lady's unfortunate death. I think, perhaps,' he added, 'that you knew Miss Gregory?'

There was a silence, then Aunt Bess said, 'Indeed I knew her. A lady of great distinction. Her father was a Writer to the Signet and in her younger days she was well known in

151

society. She gave generously towards good causes.'

'After the lady's death,' Jamie went on, 'the lawyer, Mr Humbie, offered Miss Dunlop a post as companion to a young lady in Fife, and that is how she became involved in these unfortunate events.'

'Mr Humbie—I know him well. He comes to my soirées,' his aunt said lightly.

'I fear,' Jamie told her, 'that he will not be attending soirées for some time.'

'He is in jail, Mother,' Rosa put in, eager to be part of the drama. 'Jamie has just told me.'

'Impossible,' Aunt Bess said with a frown. 'Such a gentleman. There must have been a grave mistake. I will see what I can do. I will speak to my lawyer.' There was a pause as she realised that her lawyer was Mr Humbie.

Eliza had been silent until now, but suddenly she felt that she had been discussed long enough. She felt embarrassed for Jamie, having to plead her cause to his aunt.

'I am sorry to intrude, madam,' she said. 'I can well understand that it is an imposition to have a stranger arrive without warning, and in such a state.' She grimaced as she looked down at her crumpled skirts, which were stained with sea water. She was aware, too, that the smell of fish must still cling to her clothes.

'I am sure,' she said with as much dignity as she could, 'that if you are unable to offer me shelter, I may be able to find somewhere else,

152

and I apologise for disturbing you.'

'But of course you must stay here. Have I not already said so?' Aunt Bess said, although, in fact, she had said no such thing. 'And there is no thought of finding somewhere else, for there is not a bed to be found in the whole of the city.'

'Aunt,' Jamie interrupted, 'I am grateful to you for agreeing to have Miss Dunlop to stay for a few days.'

'This house is famed for its hospitality,' Aunt Bess said grandly. 'Besides, despite her appearance—' she sniffed as she caught the scent of fish that hung around Eliza 'you have persuaded me that she is a lady.'

With that she rose and tugged at an embroidered bell pull, and when the parlour maid appeared, she rattled out instructions. A bedroom to be prepared, a hot-water pan to be put into the bed, the cook to prepare a meal.

Rosa heaved herself off the sofa.

'I am sure I can find you clothes of mine that will fit you,' she said. 'There is still a cupboard quite full of my clothes from when I was a girl. But now,' she added, 'you can see that they are of little use to me.'

Jamie rose.

'I have errands to do,' he said. 'I thank you most sincerely, Aunt. Perhaps I may be permitted to return later and escort Miss Dunlop and yourself, if you wish, to see the King's procession and, in the evening, the

153

fireworks on Arthur's Seat.'

'Oh, I should dearly love to see the fireworks!' Rosa exclaimed. 'But perhaps it would be unwise in my present condition. I should not care for my child to be born to the sound of exploding Catherine wheels.'

Aunt Bess frowned at her daughter.

'Such levity is not becoming,' she said.

Jamie hid a grin. Rosa had not changed from the cousin he recalled as a girl; impetuous, harum-scarum, with a lively sense of fun.

When Rosa opened the cupboard containing her dresses, Eliza gasped in amazement. Such wonderful dresses. Rosa carelessly pulled out first one then another.

Eliza had never seen such finery. There were day dresses of cashmere and merino, and evening gowns of organdie and gauze. There was a pelisse in a peacock blue, fastened down the front with hooks and eyes. She admired a swansdown muff, and a row of shoes, ranging from boots to delicate evening shoes, trimmed with silk rosettes.

Eliza gasped with admiration.

'Such beautiful things,' she said. 'You are most generous to share them with me.'

'It is nothing.' Rosa smiled. 'It is very boring here, as you can imagine. I should dearly love to be out in the streets, seeing the decorations and the crowds, and the new lamps. Oh, I would love to go to one of the balls in the

154

King's honour. The gentlemen will look so splendid. Full Highland dress, with steel-wrought pistols, broadsword and dirk. The ladies attending the ball are to approach with their trains carried over one arm until they reach the King's presence. And they must have at least nine feathers in each headdress.' She smiled. 'As you can imagine, Mamma has been in a state of indecision, trying on one headdress after another.' She went on, 'Oh, how I would enjoy all the festivities!

'But at least I am in Edinburgh amid all the excitement. Mamma insisted I stay with her while Henry was in the city with his regiment. It would not be safe for me to be at home when I might be confined any day.' She made a face. 'Mamma would not like to miss the birth of her first grandchild. And with the drama of the King's visit, she is quite beside herself with excitement!' Rosa laughed.

'But,' Eliza consoled her, 'it will be quite different when your baby is born. Then you will have the pleasure of motherhood and showing the child to all your friends and relations.'

'That is so.' Rosa began to cheer up. 'And I hope it will not be long. Meantime,' she said, 'do make your choice. You are welcome to take any of these dresses.' She went on briskly. 'You will need a day dress, and something for evening.' She produced a cream silk dress embroidered with flowers, the hem trimmed

155

with a flounce. 'And shoes,' she went on, looking at Eliza's sturdy boots. She picked up two pairs of sandals with criss-cross lacing, and a pair of delicate kid slippers.

Eliza could hardly believe her good fortune.

One moment, she thought, she was lying, damp and cold in an evil-smelling bunk on a fishing boat. And now here she was being offered some of the most beautiful gowns she had ever seen. How her fortunes had changed!

There was but one niggle of regret. If only Jamie was more than just a good friend.

THE KING'S ARRIVAL

Jamie returned to the house that evening. He was as good as his word.

'It is now certain that the King will land at Leith tomorrow.'

Leith was a thriving seaport, with ships arriving every week from Rotterdam and Antwerp. There were cargoes too, of herrings from Wick, and grain from Dundee. And now it was even busier with the crowds who had been waiting for days to greet the King.

It would be, Jamie promised, a fine sight, with Highlanders who had come from all over the country, bands playing and fleets of small boats. It seemed all of Scotland was gathering to welcome the King.

The *Queen Margaret* steamboat was one of the first to sail out to meet the royal yacht. It was crammed with officials from the city and ladies in their best bonnets, anxiously glancing up at the skies, hoping that the rain would clear. Along the pier, scaffolding had been built to allow spectators a good view of the King's arrival.

It was almost impossible to find a place on any balcony in Edinburgh. But perhaps they could find a place on the route as the King's procession reached the city.

'Would you ladies care to go to Princes Street?' he asked. 'We should have a fine sight of the procession as it approaches up York Place and St Andrew's Street.'

Eliza could not believe her good fortune.

'I wish I could go, too,' Rosa said wistfully. 'But it is out of the question.'

'Just so,' Aunt Bess agreed firmly. 'I fear it would be too exhausting for me.' She told Jamie that he must take one of the servants with him and Eliza, for propriety.

The crowd was so dense that it was hard to see anything at all. People clustered on rooftops, hung out of windows, and climbed lampposts for a better view.

The distant sound of pipes and drums, and a low rumble of cheers, were signs that the King's procession was on the way. People waved their handkerchiefs, hats and silk flags they had bought for the occasion. At the moment when he actually passed, Eliza raised herself on her toes, and tried to see over the heads of the group in front. But all she could glimpse was a hat doffed and a hand waving, and she assumed that must be the King.

'How exciting!' she said to Jamie, not liking to confess how little she had seen. After all, he had been very kind and had gone to a great amount of trouble. The decorations in the streets were very grand—there were stars and crowns, the Royal initials and flowers. Eliza was caught up in the excitement of the occasion.

'I am sorry we did not see more,' Jamie said, as if he knew that she was trying to be polite. 'But we will go out this evening to see the fireworks and bonfire on Calton Hill. I've seen them carrying up timber and tar barrels for the bonfire. It should be a splendid sight. And, of course, you will be attending the ball at the Assembly Rooms and the King is to appear then.'

*   *   *

'You look beautiful,' Rosa said a little enviously, as Eliza pirouetted before her in the cream silk gown. 'Now you must let me arrange your hair.'

Eliza looked dubious. Her hair was straggling and looked unkempt. The damp air and the sea water had done it no good at all, and she was afraid that she would be a fright compared with many of the elegant guests.

'I will curl your hair at the front in a fringe,' Rosa said. 'And twist it into ringlets. I have often done it for my sisters.

'There,' she said after a few minutes. She held up a looking-glass in front of Eliza. 'How does that look?'

'You are a genius!' Eliza cried. 'I look quite different.' She gave Rosa an affectionate hug.

'There, you are ready,' Rosa said, smiling. 'Except you must have some jewellery.' She opened her jewellery case. 'I think this would suit.' She brought out a delicate pendant, a stone of amber mounted on a gold chain.

'But I cannot borrow that!' Eliza said. 'It is much too valuable.'

'Nonsense.' Rosa shook her head. 'It will suit you admirably. All I ask is that you describe to me when you return, everything you have seen.'

'I will notice everything to tell you,' Eliza promised.

Eliza had never seen anything like it, though she had often imagined a ball—the fiddlers, the candles, the buzz of conversation, the elegance of the dancers—and the dresses!

She could hardly tear her eyes from the wonderful gowns. Each lady arriving at the door seemed to be more elegant than the rest.

'Dressmakers in Edinburgh were not to be outdone,' Rosa had told her. 'For weeks now they have been working hard to produce dresses fit for a Royal visit. Many ladies have had gowns made of plaid for daytime. And as well as the dressmakers, the weavers have been busy—we now have many beautiful Paisley shawls!'

Eliza was amazed. She noticed one lady in a primrose yellow Grecian-style gown, with a draped tunic, white gloves and a dainty reticule. Some of the older ladies wore ostrich feather headdresses, many with diamonds. Others wore elegant net gowns with a long train of satin in a contrasting shade.

Many of the younger guests wore slim gowns of silk or satin, trimmed with artificial flowers, with puffed sleeves.

Aunt Bess looked magnificent. Her deep gold satin gown had a long train which she swept over her arm, ready to let the train down at the correct moment, so that she might sweep a low curtsy to the King. The white ostrich plumes on her headdress did not look secure and they nodded wildly as she turned from one friend to another, greeting everyone with whom she had any acquaintance. Her feet were in the fashionable Roman sandals, laced up the front, and so tightly tied that she was almost unable to walk. She carried a small ivory fan, and a reticule made of matching silk.

Jamie turned to Eliza with a smile.

'Let us escape the chaperones,' he whispered.

Eliza glanced towards Aunt Bess, who had hardly watched the dancers. She was deep in conversation with her friends, the ostrich plumes on her bonnet nodding vigorously as she told an especially juicy piece of scandal. The ladies beside her gaped in astonishment as she imparted yet another item of gossip.

'Come.' Jamie took Eliza's hand and led her towards a secluded part of the hall where they would not be seen. 'We should be outside in a flowery garden,' he said with a wry smile. 'Moonlight and the scent of roses and the distant hooting of an owl. It is most unseasonable weather.'

'How very poetic,' Eliza said. Outside the rain was beating down and a small group who had waited to protest about the King's visit had long since gone home, dispirited.

Why, Eliza wondered, was Jamie suddenly so nervous? It was not like him to be hesitant. She smiled encouragingly at him. Strange, she thought, how she had known Jamie only a little time, and yet she felt she knew him well. He was not particularly handsome, but had an engaging smile.

'I am a struggling lawyer,' he said, still in that hesitant way. 'And will be for a little time to come. But I am determined to make my way.'

'I have no doubt,' Eliza said kindly, 'that you will become a distinguished lawyer. I can see you rising to the heights of your profession.'

'You honour me.' He shook his head. 'I will spend the next few years making wills for difficult people and settling disputes. But,' he said quickly, 'let's have no talk of wills and disputes. I have always wanted,' he went on, 'someone with whom to share my life. Someone who is beautiful, and brave, too. Someone to love and cherish as she deserved.'

Eliza was silent. Of course he meant Catriona. She thought of her friend's serene expression, her creamy complexion, her red-gold curls. Yes, she was certainly beautiful. And brave, too. She remembered how Catriona's hand had trembled as she tried to fasten Eliza's old woollen cloak. Yet there had been no word of the terror she must have felt.

And how she had captivated the family at the manse. She remembered how tenderly Jamie had cared for her. No wonder Jamie had fallen in love with her.

Well, if Catriona was Jamie's choice, she thought, I will be glad for her. She will be like a sister to me and we will always be good friends. But if only . . .

'You and Catriona,' she said.

'Catriona?' Jamie said. 'What about Catriona?'

'I thought you and she . . .' Eliza began. 'I thought you had a tenderness for her.'

'Catriona?' He frowned. 'But do you not know what she means to do?'

Eliza, confused, shook her head.

'She has not spoken to you?'

Eliza shook her head.

'Well, perhaps she wants to be certain, but I know she will tell you. She has talked with my father, and he has encouraged her. She means to go back to Belgium and join the order of nuns at the convent where she stayed, and become a helper, caring for the sick. She will return very soon.'

'I am very glad for her,' Eliza said. She remembered how Catriona had cared for Kate, how gentle she had been. And how she had not minded in the least washing the sick woman and tending to her needs.

Jamie seemed as if he was about to say something, then hesitated.

'And you?'

'I have no special plans,' Eliza said hastily. 'But surely someone will employ me as a companion.' She was not going to think about that tonight. This was to be an evening to remember.

'Eliza,' he said, 'I have something I wish to say to you.'

'Jamie!' At that moment a friend of Aunt Bess put her head round the corner. 'Ah, there you are!' she said archly. 'I am sent by your aunt to ask you to return to the dancing. She wishes that you would dance with the elder Miss Grant.'

'I am otherwise engaged,' Jamie replied stiffly.

163

'She was quite insistent,' the friend said, clearly very much in awe of Aunt Bess.

Jamie stifled a grin.

'Please,' Eliza interrupted, 'you must go to your aunt. I have taken up enough of your time.'

He bowed.

'We shall have the next dance after this,' he said. 'And we will talk again.'

'Certainly.' Eliza smiled. But she knew that the moment had passed.

A STOWAWAY

Robbie was such a regular visitor to the manse that Maggie was surprised when one morning he did not appear at the usual time for his lessons.

'Have you seen anything of Robbie, my dear?' The minister appeared at the door of his study, his finger marking the place in the book he was reading. 'Should he not be here by now?'

Maggie glanced at the grandfather clock.

'He should be here.' Robbie was not the most eager of scholars. He still had difficulty in reading and writing, and Joshua Grieve had doubts whether he would ever master simple arithmetic. As for Latin, he had realised some time ago that the boy, though bright and intelligent, had no aptitude for languages. He knew very well that Robbie had no interest in his books, and looked forward to the moment the lesson would end. Then he would escape rapidly to the kitchen, where there might be a fresh bannock with butter waiting for him.

The minister had tried to explain how important it was that Robbie should learn his letters.

'If you want to be an apprentice, then you must know how to read and how to reckon figures,' he had said. But Robbie took no notice, and the minister came to the conclusion that he was wasting his time. However, he liked the boy and found his impudence engaging, and continued doing his best to teach Robbie something at least.

So now he was puzzled that there was no sign of the boy. He was usually very punctual.

'I hope that Kate is not ill again,' Maggie said anxiously. 'But then Robbie would have come for me, I'm sure.' She went on, 'Don't worry, Father. As soon as I have washed the pots, I will go down to Kate's and see what has happened to him.'

A quarter of an hour later, she hurried down the hill, along the main street and turned into the vennel.

'Oh, Miss Maggie!' Kate turned from the sink. 'I am thankful you've come. Sandy is away and I had no-one to send to you.'

'It's about Robbie,' Maggie said. 'He has

not come for his lesson, and we hoped that you were not ill again.'

'I'm some better,' Kate said. 'But that wee mischief—see what I'll dae to him when he comes hame.'

'He's not been back here?' Maggie looked round the room.

'He's not been hame all night.' Kate burst into a wail.

Maggie's heart sank, but she tried not to let Kate see that she, too, was anxious.

'It is not like Robbie,' she said carefully.

'And he's always hame,' Kate cried. 'He never misses coming back for his meal.'

Where had he gone, Maggie wondered. The most likely place was the harbour.

She put an arm round Kate's shoulders.

'I will go to the harbour and see if anyone has had sight of him,' she said.

'If only Sandy was home,' Kate said, mopping her eyes. 'That laddie's beyond me, and I promised my mother I would look after him.'

'Never fear,' Maggie told her, more confidently than she felt. 'I'm sure he will be back soon.'

She made her way down to the harbour, stepping carefully along the quay, and trying to avoid tripping over coiled ropes. There were curious glances from some of the fishermen and one called out, 'Are you looking for somebody, miss?'

'A boy. Robbie,' Maggie replied. 'He's often here.'

The man shook his head.

'I havena seen him today. He's down here most days.'

'If you should see him, tell him to go right back home,' Maggie said firmly.

But she felt despondent. What had happened to Robbie?

She continued walking the length of the quay, looking carefully at each boat as she passed. By now her first anger at Robbie had passed and she was becoming more anxious with every moment.

And then she stopped. Surely this was Captain Hansen's boat. It was as trim as she might have expected, brass gleaming, hull newly painted.

She leaned over the wall.

'Is Captain Hansen about?'

'He's gone up to the village. He will not be long,' one of the crew called out. 'Can I be of help?'

'May I come aboard?' Maggie asked. She explained quickly about Robbie's disappearance.

The man looked doubtful.

'I have not seen a boy,' he said. 'But you may search, if you wish.' He held out a hand to Maggie, and she kilted her skirts and climbed down the ladder and on to the boat.

They searched through the bunks, the

wheelhouse, the narrow galley.

'He is not here,' Maggie admitted, disappointed.

'There is one bunk,' the man said, 'that is not used. It was for one of the crew who cannot sail with us.'

Maggie felt a sudden spurt of hope.

'May I look?'

She stretched up into the topmost bunk and reached under the rough blanket.

'Robbie!' She flung off the blanket and stared at the forlorn figure lying underneath.

'How long have you been here?'

He stared at her.

'I came last night. They're a man short. I want to go with them . . .' his voice faltered.

'Get down!' Maggie grabbed him by his collar. 'Your sister is frantic with anxiety. Come down this instant!'

Meekly, he did as he was told.

'Thank you.' Maggie turned to the seaman. 'I am sorry you have been troubled.'

'He wanted to go to sea?' The man smiled. 'Well, maybe one day when he is older.'

Maggie half-pushed, half-dragged Robbie on to the quay and marched him along. On the way, they met Captain Hansen holding a sheaf of papers, who stopped in surprise.

'Miss Maggie!'

'I am very sorry, Captain Hansen,' Maggie said. 'This wretch has been hiding on your boat.'

'Ah!' The captain hid a smile, unsuccessfully. 'He wanted to go to sea.'

'So it seems. And now I am taking him home.' Maggie gave the boy a shake.

'Do not be too hard on him, Miss Maggie,' the captain said. 'I, too, stowed away when I was a lad, and was discovered in time.' He smiled at her. 'I hope I shall see you before we sail in a few days' time?'

Maggie was a little confused by this. Holding firmly on to Robbie's collar, she said, 'Well, yes, indeed. I hope so. You must excuse me, his sister is quite beside herself with worry.'

'Indeed. It is a good thing he was discovered. And if he has been hiding all night, he must be hungry.'

'I'm starving,' Robbie burst out.

'It is your own fault.' Maggie gave him another shake. 'Goodbye, Captain Hansen.'

The captain watched her as she marched the unfortunate Robbie homewards.

'What a woman!' he said to himself. 'What a woman!'

During that week, Maggie and Catriona had spent a good deal of time with Kate and her family

'You are too good,' Catriona had said to her friend. 'Now Kate is almost well again, and Robbie is found, perhaps you do not need to go down there so often?' she added a little slyly.

169

'Oh,' Maggie had said in an offhand way, 'there is always something to be done for Kate.'

'Very well.' Catriona had smiled. 'I can help with the mending.'

There was always a warm welcome from Kate.

'You should not do so much for us,' she exclaimed, emptying the basket that Maggie had brought from the manse garden.

There was indeed not much to do that morning, or during the following days. Kate had swept the kitchen with her usual care and had scrubbed the deal table.

While Catriona took out her sewing basket, and began to mend a shirt of Robbie's, Maggie swept up the baby and began crooning to him.

'There cam a man tae our town, tae our town, to our town. And his name was Wully Wood . . .'

The child clapped his hands as she continued.

She ended the song, 'And he ate up a' the bawbee baps, and his name was Aiken Drum.' She jiggled the baby on her knee and he crowed with delight.

'Well sung!' a voice said from the door. Maggie looked up, blushing.

'Captain Hansen. I did not know you were there.'

'I merely called in to enquire about young Robbie,' he said. 'I trust he is none the worse for his adventure.'

'I thank you. He is quite recovered,' Maggie said.

'We were grateful to you,' Kate added. 'I dinna ken whit would hae happened to him had he no' been found.'

'I hope you were not too hard on him,' the captain said. 'Ah, well, I shall see him soon.' But he made no move to go, and instead sat down beside Maggie. 'You have a fine voice, Miss Maggie,' he said. 'And I think that is an old Scots song.'

Maggie forgot to be shy.

'Yes, my father collects old Scots songs, and has sung them to us since my brother and I were very young.'

'I could happily sit here all day, listening to you,' the captain admitted. He rose to go.

'I must take my leave.' He bowed to Kate. 'But may I return? And perhaps you will be here, Miss Maggie, and will sing some more of those nursery songs.'

'Perhaps,' Maggie replied a little distantly, not liking to appear too forward.

After he had gone, Catriona said, 'Well, I think he is much—'she fumbled for a word '—taken with you.'

'Oh, nonsense.' Maggie leaned nearer the fire to hide her blushes. 'He is only being gentlemanly.' But somehow she did not sing the next song with the same enthusiasm.

Maggie had not forgotten Eliza, but she was

thankful to hear from Jamie that she was well and safe and would be returning to Kingsferry in a few days. There was a great deal to be told, she knew, and she would just have to be patient till Eliza came home.

Oddly enough, though she knew Eliza had attended a ball in the King's honour, and had seen the fireworks and the processions, she did not envy her.

'Now that is strange,' she said to herself herself, 'when I have always longed for a life of splendour and luxury.' But she pushed the thought aside.

She found she was making excuses to visit Kate and her family. Perhaps there was a bag of beans from the garden, or a bunch of the minister's roses to deliver. While sitting in the now-familiar kitchen, she would find herself watching the door for the shadow of a large figure, and listening for a voice she now recognised

'Captain Hansen!' she would greet him as if surprised. One day he sat down on the oak settle by the fireside. 'This must be only a short visit,' he said. 'We sail in two days and I will be away for some weeks.'

'Oh!' Maggie's hand flew to her mouth, and then, embarrassed, she tried to hide her dismay.

'But I will return soon,' he said, smiling at her. 'To visit my good friends, Sandy and Mistress Kate, and I hope to see you, Miss

Maggie, and your friend, Miss Catriona.'

'Yes, indeed.' Maggie was flustered. 'We shall look forward to seeing you.'

He did not stay long.

'Maybe I will bring some plaything for the little one when I come back to Kingsferry.'

He turned to Kate and Maggie.

'Goodbye, my friends. Until my next visit.' Then he hesitated, and said to Maggie in a low voice. 'Perhaps you would direct me to your father's house, Miss Maggie?'

Maggie looked surprised and started to explain.

'Oh, I am so foolish about finding the way,' he interrupted. 'If we go outside, perhaps you can tell me which way to turn.'

The vennel outside was empty but for a boy running along the way, unsuccessfully trying to control a hoop.

'You turn right at the end of this lane,' Maggie began. 'But,' she said, 'why do you wish to know the way to the manse?'

'I am foolish about finding the way,' he said again.

Maggie laughed.

'And you are a sea captain!' she exclaimed. 'I should not like to be in any ship steered by you.'

'I had rather hoped you might,' he said, looking confused. Then he added in a rush, 'Miss Maggie, I wish to see your father to ask his permission to court you.'

173

'Well!' Maggie was surprised, confused and delighted all at once. 'But why?'

'Ever since I saw you sitting by that fireside, singing to the little one, I thought,' he said, 'I thought you beautiful.' He paused. 'I am not good at fancy speeches, at talking of love, as other suitors might. But I do hope that your father will allow me to court you.'

'It is my decision,' Maggie told him. 'Not my father's, though of course I respect him.'

'And your decision?' he said, smiling.

Maggie became confused.

'I don't know,' she said. 'In any case, you hardly know me,' she protested, common sense taking over. 'You have seen me only a few times. You do not know me at all.'

'I know enough.' He took her hand. 'Miss Maggie, I must go. Will you come to the harbour tomorrow and wish me godspeed?'

'But of course!' Maggie cried. 'And I hope you will return safe.'

She watched him as he strode off down the lane. At the end, he turned and waved his hat. She waved back, then stood for a few moments, surprised by this feeling of happiness, before she turned away and went indoors.

BACK TO KINGSFERRY

Eliza could hardly believe that Kingsferry looked exactly the same. Nothing had changed since she had been kidnapped, forced into a fishing boat and rescued on the quay at Leith. She might have expected that the village itself had changed. Perhaps it might have looked less foreboding, now that she did not have to look behind her at every step. But there was no change at all, as far as she could see.

This time the sea trip from Leith to Inverkeithing had been calm. Eliza shivered as she recalled the terrifying events of just a few days ago—the smell of decaying fish, the bonds chafing at her wrists, the blindfold. Oh, it had been terrifying!

'I am fortunate,' she told herself, 'to have survived and I might not have.' Then she remembered Jamie taking her to his aunt's home, the hospitality Bess had shown, and how generous Rosa had been in lending those beautiful clothes! When Eliza left, Rosa had insisted on giving her the evening gown. 'A small present,' she had said.

A remembrance of her visit. Eliza recalled, a little sadly, the wonderful evening of the ball. Dancing with Jamie in the cotillions and quadrilles. The splendour of the ladies' dresses, the glimpse of Sir Walter Scott and a sight of the King. There, Eliza remembered, she had been a little disappointed. Surely the stout figure in the kilt with the pink leggings was not the regal figure of her imagination.

It had been a wonderful few days. So many astonishing things had happened, not least Jamie's news that Catriona planned to return to Belgium to the convent.

Eliza knew she would be welcome at the manse for as long as she cared to stay, but she was determined not to impose on the kindness of her friends.

As she made her way up the hill towards the manse, her spirits rose. Oh, it had been pleasant staying in the grand house in Charlotte Square, and being waited on. She had enjoyed the splendid meals, the air of comfort. But it was not for her, she thought, and she looked forward to the more homely manse with books and papers everywhere, a smell of cooking, of barley broth and oatmeal bannocks.

She pulled at the bell rope and the little maid answered. At that moment, Maggie appeared from the sitting-room.

'You need not ring as if you were a visitor,' she scolded Eliza. 'Oh, it is good to see you again. Come in and tell us all about those great events in Edinburgh.' She led the way into the sitting-room.

Catriona, in a chair by the window, rose and gave Eliza a warm hug.

'I am so glad to be able to thank you,' she said. 'But for you I would have been kidnapped and taken to Edinburgh. I cannot think that I would have lived through such a dreadful experience.'

'Indeed it was nothing. It is Jamie we have to thank. He found out what was happening and informed the authorities, and he was there at the quay to rescue me when the boat was tied up. It was all most exceedingly well done.'

Catriona smiled and picked up the dress that Maggie had discarded.

'I will finish this for you,' she said, and shook her head over Maggie's huge stitches.

'We hope to see my brother soon,' Maggie said. 'He is to be in the district, visiting someone to deal with a family matter. Something about a will, I think.'

Eliza felt a little flutter of excitement. Jamie would be arriving soon. She said, as casually as she could, 'It will be very pleasant to see your brother again. He was most kind to me, and escorted me to a ball in the Assembly Rooms.'

'Do tell us all,' Maggie probed. 'I long to know what the ladies were wearing. I'm sure they were most elegant.'

'Indeed they were.' Eliza tried to describe that glittering evening.

'And the King—did you see him?' Maggie asked.

'He looked very grand, very fine.' There was no point in shattering her friend's illusions.

Better she should keep the image of a regal, imposing figure than hear the true description of a stout figure dressed in tartan, who did not look as she had imagined.

'Well, it all sounds truly magnificent.' Maggie sighed. 'I wish I could have been there. Not that life has been uneventful here,' she added with a little smile.

'I have heard from Jamie,' Eliza said to Catriona, 'that you have plans for the future.'

Catriona blushed.

'I am sorry that I did not tell you before this,' she said, 'but I was uncertain what to do. As you know, I was brought here by sea, and I had no choice. But I wished that I had been able to stay in the convent, with my dear sisters.'

Maggie interrupted.

'But Catriona was able to have a long talk with my father. Often he seems as if he does not live in the same world as us, but he is very wise and one can always ask him for advice and know that it will be sound.'

'We talked for a long time,' Catriona went on, 'and he has written to the Reverend Mother. I shall be returning soon to Belgium.' Her face lit up. 'I am so happy to be going home. I will be working with the sisters in the infirmary.' She turned to Eliza. 'But I will never forget what you have done for me.'

'I am glad for you,' Eliza told her. She remembered how gentle and caring Catriona

178

had been with Kate during her fever. She could imagine Catriona tending the sick in the convent. It was the right place for her to be.

'And what of Kate?' she asked.

'She is well,' Maggie replied cheerfully. 'Robbie is here nearly every day. He has made a great friend in Erik.'

'Erik?' Eliza looked puzzled.

'He is a Norwegian sea captain whose ship has been in the harbour. Sometimes he calls on Kate and Sandy, and Robbie . . .' she laughed, '. . . has found a new hero.'

Eliza noticed a faint blush on her friend's cheek. She knew that Maggie still spent a good deal of time at Kate's home, helping with the baby, washing the pots, and making broth.

Was that the only attraction, she wondered.

Suddenly Eliza felt very much alone. Here were Maggie and Catriona, both with life opening up before them. And as for her, she had no-one. No-one who cared for her.

She wondered what she could do. There must be large houses in the neighbourhood where a companion might be welcome, she thought.

Still, she tried to smile for Catriona's sake.

'I am truly glad for you,' she said. 'And I have seen what a caring nurse you are. I know the nuns will welcome you back again.'

'And Robbie,' Maggie began with a smile, 'you know how he has longed to go to sea. He hardly talks of anything else. Kate has been anxious for him—a fisherman's life is a dangerous one. But he is set on it. And Erik—I mean Captain Hansen—has talked a good deal to Robbie about his voyages. He has sailed to the Arctic . . .'

Her voice trailed off, but not before Eliza had noticed that faint blush when her friend spoke of the Norwegian captain.

It was a merry evening at the manse. Maggie cooked a fowl, and there was a lemon posset to follow. The minister was kind and welcoming.

'We are glad to see you safely back with us,' he told Eliza. 'We must thank God for your deliverance.' He laid a hand on Eliza's head. 'We hope you will stay with us for a very long time.'

But would she? Eliza's thoughts were in a whirl. So much had happened in a few short weeks, it was much too early to plan her future. But she knew she must come to a decision.

It was not fair, she told herself, to be a burden to the family at the manse, who had little enough. So, she decided, the next day she would make enquiries in the district. Surely there was someone who would employ her as a companion. Though she couldn't help feeling downcast at the thought. Running to and fro, fetching and carrying, playing endless games of cards. She sighed.

Suddenly, she decided that perhaps her head would be clearer if she took a short walk in the fresh air. She looked round enquiringly. 'Would anyone else care for a walk?'

'Please excuse me.' Catriona looked up from working on a lace border. 'I want to finish this.'

'And I have chores to do for tomorrow,' Maggie added. 'We expect Jamie to arrive on the coach quite early.'

'No matter,' Eliza replied agreeably. 'I will take a short walk while it is still light.'

'Will you be safe on your own?' the minister asked a little anxiously.

'I will be perfectly safe,' Eliza assured him. 'No harm can come to me here.' Then she laughed. 'Not now, at any rate.'

She set off down the hill, and instead of going on to the harbour, turned off at the lane towards Shore House.

Looking up at the windows, she remembered that evening she had arrived. It seemed a long time ago now. The windows had been hung with net curtains that had not been washed for some time, the paintwork on the door and windows was flaking, and there had been a general air of neglect.

She paused, looking up at the house. Nothing had changed, except the shutters were now closed, and there were no candles burning upstairs. A few wisps of paper blew around the front doorstep. Was anyone there, she wondered.

She turned and leaned over the wall,

gazing out at a small fishing boat ploughing steadfastly through the waves, and at the lights on the far shore. How still it seemed, with no sign of habitation in Shore House, and no-one walking along the shore.

Eliza stood there for some minutes, enjoying the peace of the summer evening. But then she began to feel chilled, and wrapped her shawl more tightly around her.

'Good evening! I hope I don't intrude.'

Eliza whirled round.

'What a fright you gave me! I thought . . .'

'I am sorry. You thought I might be the stranger who haunted Shore House,' Jamie said.

'Nothing of the kind,' Eliza replied sharply. 'But anyone would be alarmed by such a sudden appearance.'

'I am truly sorry,' he apologised again. 'But I have only just arrived and my sister told me I might find you here.'

'I was just walking for a breath of air,' Eliza explained.

'In that case, may I accompany you? It would be safer, perhaps.'

'I do not know,' Eliza said, 'why everyone seems to think I cannot look after myself.'

'Nothing of the kind,' Jamie defended. 'We are simply anxious for your welfare.'

Immediately Eliza felt ashamed of having spoken so abruptly. Jamie and his family had been so kind to her, and she knew she owed her life to Jamie. Had he not rescued her from the boat at Leith, she might very well have been thrown overboard.

'Thank you,' she said. 'You have all been so kind to me.'

She glanced up at the shuttered windows of Shore House.

'I do not know,' she said contritely, 'how I would have managed had it not been for you and Maggie and your father. And,' she hesitated, 'what would have happened to me at Leith, when they found I was not Catriona.' She shuddered.

'It was nothing.' Jamie smiled at her. 'And you need not have nightmares about the Shore House, for Mistress Kilbain has gone.'

'Gone where?'

'No-one knows. But so I was told by Robbie.'

'How well informed he is!' Eliza interrupted, smiling.

'Well,' Jamie went on, 'Robbie had been keeping a watch on Shore House, and one morning last week he saw a carriage draw up at the door, and Mistress Kilbain hurried out, carrying her bags, got into the carriage and was driven away at great speed.'

He added, 'I gather from my sister that the tradesmen are mighty displeased, as their bills have not been paid, nor are they likely to receive their money.'

'But . . .' Eliza was puzzled, 'is there no

forwarding address? She has told no-one where she has gone?'

'No-one at all. And the stranger in black is gone, too. He was seen boarding one of the small boats that left the harbour under cover of darkness to sail on one of the contraband vessels returning to France.

'So you see,' he went on, 'you have no need to be afraid any more.'

'I am not afraid,' Eliza said, and indeed she found that she was not in the least apprehensive. Now there was no need to look over her shoulder. Kingsferry in the peaceful dusk no longer looked threatening.

Now, despite the excitement of the day, she did not feel as tired as before, but pleasantly at ease in Jamie's company. She hardly noticed that the evening was becoming chilly, and a mist was gathering. They walked on for a little in silence, then Eliza said, 'You have business in the district, I understand.'

'For a day or two. A client wishes to change his will and disinherit his family. I am sent to take his instructions, which might have changed by the time I see him tomorrow.'

He turned to her.

'I have another purpose for my visit.' He took her hand. 'Eliza, I tried when we were at the ball in the Assembly Rooms to tell you how I felt about you, and now I have another chance. I am not good at speeches, except when I stand in court, and now I have nothing to say in my own defence.' He drew a deep breath. 'I will only say that I would be honoured if you would be my wife.'

'But,' Eliza was surprised. 'You do not know me.'

'I know enough,' he said. 'I know that you are brave and honest and beautiful, and that you are the one woman with whom I could share my life.'

'But,' Eliza began again, 'I am not fit to be anyone's wife, let alone someone like you, who will one day be a distinguished lawyer. Your aunt and family are grand people in society. They would not welcome someone like me, of no background.'

'My aunt does not choose my wife for me,' he said. 'It would not matter if you were a tinker girl or a fisher lass, if you were my choice.'

'But,' Eliza protested, 'Catriona—I thought . . .'

'I have told you already,' he said, 'Catriona is nothing to me, except as a friend. She has no interest in me, nor I in her. Indeed it was Catriona who advised me to try again.'

'But,' Eliza began, and Jamie took her by the shoulders.

'I have heard enough of your buts,' he said firmly. 'Either you will marry me or you will not. If you will, then I shall do my best to make you happy, though I fear we may argue a great deal. If you will not, then there is nothing more

185

to be said. So which is it to be, yes or no?'

Looking up at him, into his kind, loving face, Eliza knew immediately that she loved Jamie and she could not bear to think of a future without him.

'Yes,' she said simply. 'Oh, yes.'

Jamie swept her into his arms, and from that moment the tall, dark hero of Eliza's imagination vanished into the mist that swept in from the sea, and she never dreamed of him again.